REDSKIN

Charlie, the young grandson of a prominent rancher, had been taken hostage by a band of vicious Cheyennes after they had slaughtered his parents. The search party forced Charlie to act as their scout. Charlie was an Indian forced by whites to pursue other Indians! If he failed, he knew they would kill him. But even if he succeeded, over the incredible odds, would they really ever accept him as anything other than a redskinned outcast?

A series of bloody events along a treacherous trail and the sympathy of a young white woman, also a victim of Indian brutality, would only add to the unpredictability of the outcome.

Lewis B. Patten wrote more than ninety Western novels in thirty years and three of them won Spur Awards from the Western Writers of America and the author himself the Golden Saddleman Award. Indeed, this highlights the most remarkable aspect of his work: not that there is so much of it, but that so much of it is so fine. Patten was born in Denver, Colorado, and served in the U.S. Navy 1933–1937. He was educated at the University of Denver during the war years and became an auditor for the Colorado Department of Revenue during the 1940s. It was in this period that he began contributing significantly to Western pulp magazines, fiction that was from the beginning fresh and unique and revealed Patten's lifelong concern with the sociological and psychological effects of group psychology on the frontier. He became a professional writer at the time of his first novel, *Massacre at White River* (1952). The dominant theme in much of his fiction is the notion of justice, and its opposite, injustice. In his first novel it has to do with exploitation of the Ute Indians, but as he matured as a writer he explored this theme with significant and poignant detail in small towns throughout the early West. Crimes, such as rape or lynching, were often at the centre of his stories. When the values embodied in these small towns are examined closely, they are found to be wanting. Conformity is always easier than taking a stand. Yet, in Patten's view of the American West, there is usually a man or a woman who refuses to conform. Among his finest titles, always a difficult choice, surely are *A Killing at Kiowa* (1972), *Ride a Crooked Trail* (1976), and his many fine contributions to Doubleday's Double D series, including *Villa's Rifles* (1977), *The Law at Cottonwood* (1978), and *Death Rides a Black Horse* (1978). His later books include *Tincup in the Storm Country* (1996), *Trail to Vicksburg* (1997), *Death Rides the Denver Stage* (1999), and *The Woman at Ox-Yoke* (2000).

REDSKIN

Lewis B. Patten

GUNSMOKE

This hardback edition 2007
by BBC Audiobooks Ltd
by arrangement with
Golden West Literary Agency

ISBN 978 1 405 68151 3

British Library Cataloguing in Publication Data available.

Printed and bound in Great Britain by
Antony Rowe Ltd., Chippenham, Wiltshire

Redskin

Chapter 1

Charlie Waymire could see them coming from a long way off because he was up greasing a windmill twenty feet off the ground. It was early October and the air was crisp, the sky blue and cloudless for as far as a man could see. Near as he could tell, there were five in the group, and they were pushing their horses hard.

He stopped work and watched, wiping his hands on a rag. They were still a quarter mile away when he began recognizing them. Joe Savage, the sheriff, rode in the lead, stocky and thick, sticking to his saddle like his pants were glued to it. Jimmy Welch, his young deputy was with him. Refugio Martinez, who worked for Jake Conger, rode behind Welch, and behind the sheriff came Jake Conger, loose and easy in the saddle, but old and bony and gray. Beside Conger rode Bart Tolliver, his foreman, a dark and quarrelsome man who never smiled and who was universally disliked.

The group pulled their plunging horses to a halt at the windmill's base. Bart Tolliver yelled in a harsh, demanding voice, "Come down off of there, you redskin sonofabitch!"

Charlie Waymire stopped wiping his hands. Anger surged in him, as sudden and explosive as a prairie fire in dry grass. He said evenly, "Why don't you try coming up after me, white man?"

Tolliver drew his gun. Joe Savage didn't turn his head, but his voice was like a whip. "Oh for God's sake, put that thing away!"

Tolliver scowled at him, but he slid the revolver back into its holster. Charlie Waymire looked down at Savage. "What the hell is this all about?"

Savage didn't like looking up. He said, "Come on down, Charlie. I want to talk to you."

"What about?" Charlie was growing wary now. He was

7

twenty-five, and a full-blood Cheyenne. Old Bill Waymire had picked him up wandering around on the prairie fifteen years before, wounded, burning with fever and plumb out of his head. Bill took him home and put him to bed. He cured him and, because he didn't know how to return him to his people, kept him, thinking maybe they'd come after him.

But no one ever had. So Charlie grew up on Bill Waymire's ranch, taking Waymire's name and the name "Charlie" which Waymire gave to him. He had grown into a strange mixture of Indian and white. He could track like an Indian, and he was reserved, withdrawn with whites other than old Bill. But he could do a white man's work. He could repair a mowing machine or grease a windmill. He could work cattle as well as any ranch hand for a hundred miles. He could break the wild broncs he and Bill caught forty or fifty miles back in the badlands during the wintertime. Better still, he broke them gentle so that they weren't spiritless when he was through with them.

Savage said impatiently, "Damn it, what difference does it make what about? Come on down. I want to talk to you."

Stubbornly Charlie insisted, "What about? I'm busy and I don't much care about coming down before I'm through."

Tolliver growled, "I'll get the redskinned bastard down offa there, Sheriff."

Savage turned his head. "Shut up. Your mouth has already made trouble enough."

Tolliver growled something that Charlie Waymire couldn't hear. In an impatient voice, Savage said, "All right! The Cheyennes burned out the Rutherfords. We found all the bodies but that of the boy, and Jake's damn near out of his mind."

Charlie suddenly understood Tolliver's use of the word "redskin." And once more, as he had a hundred times before in his life, he felt the old tug of conflict. He was white enough to be shocked and angered at the pitiless brutality of the Indians in attacking an unprotected ranch. But he was Indian enough to understand the seething anger of the young braves over the white man's long record of betrayals, lies, murders and injustices.

Shrugging, he stuck the greasy rag in the hip pocket of his pants, grabbed the rope handle of the grease can and began his descent, awkwardly because he only had the full use of one of his hands and the partial use of the other one.

His horse was tied to the windmill base. Charlie hung the grease can on the saddle horn and turned toward the sheriff, once more wiping his hands on the greasy rag. Looking up at Savage he asked warily, "What do you want with me?"

Savage glanced at Jake Conger and Jake said, "I figure they've got the boy." As if he hated asking the opinion of an Indian he asked, "What do you figure they'll do with him?"

"They won't hurt him, if that's what's worrying you. Some family will take him in and raise him like he was their own."

"What if he puts up a fight?"

Charlie Waymire shrugged. "Won't make any difference. They'll admire his spirit, that's all."

Jake Conger said, "I want him back. They killed his pa and my daughter and my older grandson. Danny's all that I've got left."

"What's that got to do with me?"

Savage broke in, "You're an Indian. You know how they think and you know what they'll most likely do. Besides that, you're probably the best tracker for two hundred miles. Only one I know that might be better is Domingo Garcia and he lives clear over in Pueblo."

Charlie said, "Maybe going after the boy isn't smart. If you start pushing them they might kill him to keep him from being seen. He's living proof they burned out Rutherfords'."

Jake growled, "Better dead than raised like them goddam savages!"

Savage asked, "Will you go?"

Charlie Waymire shook his head. "Get somebody else."

Tolliver broke in intemperately, "What the hell do you mean, sayin' get somebody else? You stinkin' redskin, you ain't got any choice. We ain't askin' you, we're tellin' you. You're goin' along with us if we have to tie you up an' drag you all the way."

Charlie Waymire's face didn't darken and his mouth showed no sign of tightening. But his eyes changed, taking on a glitter that made Tolliver take a backward step. Tolliver put his hand on his gun and said, "Don't you start anything with me, redskin. I'll blow your head off!"

Savage swung around, furious now himself. "Tolliver, get on your horse and get out of here! None of us is any too damn fond of Indians, but Charlie's been raised like he was white. Since he was ten anyways. I don't give a damn what you think of him, we need him."

"What makes you think he won't lead you right into their hands? He's as red underneath that skin as he is on the outside of it."

Savage fixed him with his angry glance. Grumbling, Tolliver climbed on his horse. Jake Conger hadn't said anything to restrain Tolliver and it was plain to Charlie that he couldn't bring himself to defend an Indian, even if that Indian had been raised like a white, even if he needed him. The memory of the bodies of his daughter and her family was too fresh in his mind. The only thing that had brought him here was need. Desperate, burning need. He knew if he was going to get his grandson back he needed Charlie Waymire's help.

Savage said, "Bart's right. You ain't got a choice. It's a citizen's duty to serve on a posse and if he don't, he can be thrown in jail."

Charlie stared at him, eyes still smoldering. "You're forgetting something, Sheriff. I'm not a citizen. I'm an Indian. I can't vote, or hold office. I can't even buy a beer."

Savage looked uncomfortable. Jake cleared his throat. Looking away at the horizon, he said in a voice that broke, "That boy is all that's left. I got to have him back!"

Charlie looked at the faces of the other men. They showed embarrassment. Their eyes, looking at Charlie, were cold. Charlie finally nodded reluctantly. "All right. But I got to go by an' tell Bill."

Savage started to say something, then closed his mouth. He nodded grudgingly. "All right. I guess we can't say no to that."

Charlie Waymire untied his horse from the foot of the windmill. He mounted and turned toward home.

Without looking back, he took the lead, trying to stifle his anger. He couldn't blame them, he supposed, for being incensed over the murder of the Rutherford family. Mostly, he guessed, he was angry because, after making him feel like dirt every time he went to town or had anything to do with any of them, they would come to him like this, not only asking him for his help but demanding it.

Savage did not range up alongside, nor did any of the others. Nobody, in fact, spoke to him. He rode at the head of the group, alone, and knew that on the pursuit, he would ride the same way, alone. He'd eat alone and he'd sleep off by himself. They'd speak to him only when it was necessary, but there would be no friendly dialogue.

The Waymire ranch house was two miles from the windmill. While he was still half a mile away, Charlie saw old Bill come out of the door and stand on the stoop, peering, a hand raised to shield his eyes from the sun.

Charie led the group into the yard, to discover that Bill held a rifle in his hands. Gray-bearded and almost as dark of face as Charlie was, Bill growled, "What the hell's goin' on?"

Savage said, "Cheyennes wiped out the Rutherfords. Burned the house an' killed everybody but Danny. They took him with them an' Charlie is goin' to help us track 'em down."

Bill looked at Charlie. "Is that right?"

Charlie nodded.

Bill looked at the faces of the men with Charlie, his old eyes as blue as the sky, faded but sharp and shrewd. He said bluntly, "Then what?"

Savage asked defensively, "What the hell do you mean, then what?"

"I mean what happens to Charlie after you find them Cheyennes? An' what if you find Danny dead?"

Savage said, "Why, hell . . ." and stopped, knowing what old Bill meant.

Bill said, "He ain't goin'."

Charlie said, "I told 'em I'd go."

"Do you know what they'll do to you if anything goes wrong?"

Charlie nodded. "I know."

"An' you still want to go?"

Charlie nodded. He wondered why, and admitted ruefully that it was because he was needed, really needed for just about the first time in his life. These men and the rest of the community might never accept him. Next best was to have them need him and have to admit it, however much it went against the grain.

Bill turned and closed the door behind him. "Then I'm goin' too. I'll get my horse." He crossed the yard to the corral.

He took his saddle down from the topmost pole, and unhooked his rope from it. He went into the corral and roped out a stocky, hammerheaded gray. He led the horse out and threw blanket and saddle on. Coming back, leading the horse, he looked up at Savage. "You folks all ready? I mean, have you got grub an' everything.?"

Savage nodded.

"Then I'll go put some things in a sack for Charlie an' me." He went into the house.

Charlie dismounted and went inside to help. He got his rifle and dumped half a box of shells for it into the side pocket of his coat. Bill was grumbling sourly as he shoved provisions into a gunnysack.

Charlie got his blanket roll and Bill's, then carried them and the rifle out. He shoved the rifle into the saddle boot and tied his blankets behind his saddle. He tied Bill's blanket roll behind Bill's saddle. By the time he had finished, Bill came out of the door, carrying the gunnysack. He tied it on and shrugged into his sheepskin coat.

Going back, he closed the door of the house, mounted, and rode to the corral. He opened the gate and chased the horses out, returning then to the waiting men. "I'm ready. Let's go."

Savage said, "We'll go to Rutherfords' so Charlie can pick up the trail."

Savage led out. Bill and Charlie dropped back to the rear of the group. Bill glanced at Charlie and said, "You doggoned fool."

Charlie grinned. "You didn't have to go either."

Bill grumbled something that Charlie couldn't understand. Bill was tough and old and hard, and in all the time he'd had Charlie, he had never once showed him any affection by word or deed.

But Charlie didn't need these outward signs. Bill had brought him home and nursed him back to life and taught him English and schooled him and showed him how to live like a white man. When Bill died, he'd leave Charlie this ranch and everything else he had.

That was enough. That was enough to make Charlie's eyes burn when he thought of it.

But there was something down deep in his gut, like a fist of ice. He had a hunch that these men, however much they needed him, weren't going to let him return when they were through with him. They were going to revenge the Rutherfords by killing him after he had helped them find the boy. Bill was only going along to try and stop them when that time came.

Chapter 2

Riding south toward the Rutherford place, Charlie Waymire avoided Bill's eyes and stared steadily at the backs of the men ahead. It wasn't hard for him to understand the hatred felt by Indians toward the whites. He hated them himself.

Six months after Bill had found him on the prairie, he had taken him to town and started him in school. Bill had already taught him enough English so that he could make himself understood. He figured the schoolmaster could take over from there.

Bill left him and rode away toward home. Charlie sat down at one of the scarred desks the way a hawk perches on a branch.

The other kids, twelve of them, turned their heads and stared at him. It made him uncomfortable because he didn't know what was in their minds. Their faces were impassive, their eyes expressionless.

At recess, he was the last one out, because he didn't quite understand what was going on. He was greeted at the door by jeers and catcalls and by the epithet he had since grown accustomed to. "Redskin." They said it like a curse, usually preceded by some adjective like "dirty" or "stinking."

He crossed the playground, trying to maintain some dignity, but feeling mighty alone. They were at his heels like a pack of dogs, pushing, knocking him down, and once they got him on the ground, pummeling him mercilessly and kicking him. Out of their mouths came all the words they had heard their parents use on Indians. They poured out on him the hate they had learned at home, not reasoning that he was only a boy and had never hurt anyone. He was an Indian, and different. His skin and hair were dark.

Charlie took it for about as long as it took him to recover from his surprise. Then he fought back. He was weak from the illness, but he fought with a ferocity that scattered them and drove them away from him. And then he counterattacked, a rock fisted in each hand. He bloodied a nose, half tore an ear loose from one boy's head, and knocked another completely out.

Now hastily, after having watched the other kids tormenting Charlie with a half smile on his mouth, the teacher intervened. He whipped Charlie with a hickory pointer and told him to leave and not to come back. Charlie went out and untied his horse. He rode away, heading not toward the Waymire ranch, but straight out across the prairie. Sooner or later he knew that he would either find some Indians or they would find him.

When he didn't show up after school, Bill went to town looking for him. Learning what had happened, Bill took his trail, stopping at dark, but going on as soon as it was light enough next day. Bill found him about noon, still-faced and sullen. He didn't force Charlie to return but he told him he wouldn't have to go to school again if he did.

Riding at a steady trot, the group reached the Rutherford place in late afternoon. The house was a blackened pile of rubble from which a thin plume of smoke still rose. The barn also had been burned. Upon the rise behind the house there were three fresh graves. Three rough wooden crosses stuck up from the heads of the graves, the names of the dead scrawled on them with charcoal taken from the rubble of the house.

Jake Conger's glance, turning toward Charlie, was cold and his face was pale. "Get going and find the trail."

Charlie considered refusing once more. He didn't because it wouldn't do him any good. He couldn't be forced to go, of course, but they'd probably kill him right here if he didn't. He rode out away from the house a ways and began a circle around the place. He found the trail and got down to study it.

There had been eight Indians, and he thought they had probably been Cheyenne. A hunting party, he supposed, composed of young men, who had attacked the Rutherford place on impulse.

Charlie studied the prints made by the Indians' horses. He was memorizing those prints the way a white man memorizes something from a printed page. He would know each horse's tracks no matter where he encountered them by the irregularities of their hoofs. Mounting, he beckoned the others, who were still sitting in the yard watching him. He waited as they rode toward him.

Bart Tolliver was the worst of the bunch, he thought. Tolliver put everything that was in his mind into words, and he'd egg the others on. But he wasn't necessarily the most dangerous. Refugio Martinez had lost his whole family to Comanches down in New Mexico. And Jimmy Welch was young and anxious to prove himself, and was therefore unpredictable.

Jake Conger and Savage would keep them from doing anything serious to him, at least until Danny Rutherford was found. But if Danny should be found dead, Charlie would pay the price. If Danny wasn't found at all, they'd probably kill Charlie in reprisal. His only chance to live was either to get away or else to find the boy, unhurt.

Bill came riding toward him. Charlie ranged out ahead of the others by forty or fifty feet, and Bill kept pace. Bill growled, "Best thing you can do is get away."

"Then they'd take it out on you."

"I can take care of myself."

"And what about the boy?"

"That ain't your lookout." Changing the subject, he asked, "What do you make of this trail?"

"Eight. Probably young men."

"Why the hell would they take the boy?"

"Knew of some family that had lost a boy about that age, I guess. Figured they'd take him back for them." A little bitterly he said, "Indians don't care what color a kid's skin is."

"How much chance you think we got of overtakin' 'em?"

"Depends on the weather some. Depends on how far they were going and on how big a village they came from. If it's very big, we haven't got nearly enough men."

Bill didn't reply. The others had now caught up. Tolliver asked suspiciously, "What the hell you two jawin' about?"

Bill swung around in his saddle. "We was talkin' about what a sonofabitch you was."

Savage broke in before Tolliver could reply, "That's enough. We got plenty of trouble without fightin' amongst ourselves."

Tolliver glared at Bill, then switched his glance to Charlie. Charlie didn't notice. His eyes were on the trail, and he urged his horse to a fast trot.

He remembered his life with the Indians, of course. He remembered an attack on their village by white soldiers. His father, mother and sister had been killed. He himself had been hurt, and he remembered an endless, pain-wracked ride on a travois. He remembered lying in a tepee recovering from his wound. And he remembered another attack by buffalo hunters. He'd crept away and escaped, and it was sometime afterward that Bill had found him, feverish and delirious. Charlie had stayed with Bill after he was well again because there was nothing for him to go back to. His family was dead. Even the small village of those who had rescued him had been destroyed. And besides, he had gotten to like Bill. The old man accepted him for what he was, without regard to the color of his skin. He treated him like he would any kid he'd picked up sick and lost. And for all his gruffness, Bill had a kind and understanding heart.

The trail lined out straight west. Charlie stayed with it until it was so dark he couldn't see it any more. Then he stopped. "We camp."

Nobody argued, although Tolliver grumbled something about the "stinkin' redskin" quitting half an hour before he had to. Charlie walked away from him. He unsaddled and picketed his horse. He walked silently toward a little brushy draw to gather wood.

He had gone no more than fifty feet before he heard running steps behind. He barely had time to turn before a charging body hit him, knocking him fifteen feet and tumbling him to the ground. Before he could get up, Tolliver stood over him. The man managed to land one solid kick in Charlie's ribs before Charlie could roll away. "Tryin' to get away, wasn't you, you redskin son-ofabitch!" Tolliver snarled.

Charlie had suddenly taken all he intended to. He got to his feet like a cat, half crouched, arms extended. Tolliver backed away two steps. He put a hand on his gun. "Oh no! You keep away from me or I'll blow a hole in you big enough to stick an arm through."

Charlie said, "Then do it," and charged the man, weaving right and left but coming on and coming fast. Tolliver yanked his gun from its holster, thumbed the hammer back and fired. The bullet tore up a geyser of sand thirty feet behind Charlie but it didn't slow him down. Tolliver got off a second shot before Charlie hit him, this one striking the ground as harmlessly as the first.

Tolliver went down, with Charlie on top of him like a mountain lion. Charlie had a knife but he didn't use it. He gripped Tolliver's thick throat with his hands, thumbs in front on the windpipe, and squeezed. Into the strength of his hands went all his anger and bitterness at the unfairness of the treatment these men had accorded him. Tolliver's face got red, then purple. He thrashed and kicked and fought. He tried to tear Charlie's hands from his throat, without success.

Dimly Charlie heard shouting voices. One was Bill's. "Charlie! Quit it now! You'll kill the sonofabitch!"

He didn't care. His hands did not relax. Tolliver's struggles began weakening. The voices kept shouting. Hands seized him and dragged him away. Between them they tore his hands from the big man's throat.

Tolliver rolled over on his belly, gagging, choking and fighting for air. Refugio Martinez slammed his rifle stock against the side of Charlie's head, making his head ring, knocking him sideways several feet. Bill yelled, "Whoa, you goddam Mex!" but Savage said, "Stand still, Waymire! Don't interfere!"

"What the hell do you mean, don't interfere? That Mex will kill him!"

"No, he won't."

The men now encircled Charlie. Martinez, coldly furious. Jimmy Welch, scared but eager. Tolliver, still fighting for breath, but anxious to get his licks in after Charlie was subdued. Conger, his eyes blazing, seeing in Charlie one of the hated breed who had killed his daughter and her family.

Martinez rushed before Charlie's head had cleared, swinging the rifle. It missed as Charlie ducked, but Jimmy flung himself at his legs and cut them out from under him.

Once he was on the ground, they all rushed in. Jimmy

straddled him, pummeling his face. Jake Conger kicked viciously at his head, missing it occasionally but connecting often enough so that Charlie's senses began to slip. Martinez was kicking at his groin. He heard Bill bawl again, "That's enough! Let him up!"

The punishment went on. Charlie knew he was going out. He knew it was possible he would not awake.

Suddenly he heard a bellow out of Bill. He heard a gunshot and the crack of a rifle barrel striking a head. Then, above him, he heard that same sound again and Jimmy Welch stopped hitting him.

He peered up, things swimming before his eyes. He saw Bill put a boot against Jimmy's chest and shove. Refugio Martinez lay on his back, unconscious, a bloody welt on his forehead. Tolliver was backing away, hands held well clear of his body. The sheriff sat on the ground, holding his head in his hands.

Bill put down a hand and Charlie took it. Bill helped him up, and steadied him. He said, "Get your horse. Get the hell out of here. You got all night."

Charlie shook his head, then winced with the throbbing pain the movement brought.

"Why not? They're goin' to kill you before they're through."

Charlie couldn't understand his own stubbornness. It was all confused. He supposed part of it was that he didn't want these white men to think they could make him run. If he did, he'd be just what they said he was.

But he also remembered the embers of the Rutherford place and the three fresh graves up there on the hill.

Besides that, he owed old Bill. For a second time Bill had saved his life. He couldn't repay him by running out on him, by leaving him to face the wrath of these five angry men. He walked to where he had left his saddle. Stooping, he got his gun and cartridge belt out of the saddlebags. He strapped the gun around his waist.

He nodded at Bill, and Bill lowered his rifle. Savage got unsteadily to his feet, looking at Bill and then at Charlie murderously. Jake Conger had the decency to look ashamed of the way he'd let his passions get the best of him.

Refugio Martinez stared at Charlie with naked hatred. Tolliver grumbled to himself and spat disgustedly on the ground. Jimmy Welch glanced toward the sheriff, whether for approval or condemnation, Charlie couldn't tell. But he knew one thing. He knew what to expect from all of them.

Chapter 3

Charlie slept little. His head ached murderously throughout the night. He stared gloomily up at the stars, aware that Conger was also awake, watching him.

Conger expected him to run first chance he got. And, he thought, if he had any sense he would.

But run to what? To Indians who would look upon him with equal suspicion and distrust, who might drive him away, or kill him? No. He would be as much an outcast in the Indian camps as he was in the white man's towns.

He would stay, then, and help them find Danny Rutherford if he could. Afterward, maybe they'd be more inclined to accept him as one of them. He doubted it, but it was a chance.

Dawn finally lightened the eastern sky and Conger got up, calling out to the others, "It's morning. Roll out. I want to get on that trail as soon as it's light enough."

The men got up. Charlie didn't try going after wood. In fact, he did nothing but saddle up his horse. Bill built a fire for the two of them. He made coffee and they drank it standing in the morning chill while bacon sizzled in a pan. When the bacon was cooked, Bill put cold biscuits into the grease and fried them. They ate, finishing before the others did. Both of them were saddled and ready by the time Savage, who was last, threw his saddle on.

Once more, Charlie led out. The trail was plain and easily followed. Any one of the men in this party could have followed it. But it wouldn't stay this plain. Already it was almost two days old. It could be wiped out by rain or wind at any time. The Indians who had made it might scatter or separate. They might join up with another traveling band, or might eventually reach their home village, where their identities would be lost except for the individuality of their horses' tracks, which were indelibly etched in Charlie Waymire's memory.

Four hours out of their night's camp, Charlie found where the Indians had halted night before last, their first camp since the attack. Seeing it ahead, Charlie raised a hand to stop the others. He dismounted and handed the reins of his horse to Bill. He advanced into the remains of the Indian camp afoot.

Conger yelled, "See Danny's tracks?"

Charlie did not immediately reply. He was studying the ground. The Indians had built a single small fire. Apparently they'd had provisions stolen from the Rutherford place before they burned it. There was a piece of bacon rind lying near the ashes of the fire. There were some raw potatoes lying around that the Indians had apparently either used to throw at each other or to play catch with.

He found Danny's tracks. The boy had, immediately upon being lifted down from his horse, tried to run away. A single brave had pursued him and brought him back. There were the marks of a scuffle where the Indian had released him and Charlie saw the mark of Danny's body where he had fallen, apparently after being struck.

He turned and called, "They had Danny and he was all right. He tried to run away and they brought him back. I guess he gave them some back sass, because one of them knocked him down."

Conger growled, "The dirty redskin bastard!"

Charlie didn't respond to that. He looked around a few moments more, searching for clues as to where the Indians might be headed, but he found nothing. He mounted and led out again.

They did not stop for dinner, but kept going without even resting the horses. About two o'clock, Charlie thought he saw a thin plume of smoke in the distance. He stopped, pointed it out, and said, "I'll go on ahead a ways and check it out."

Tolliver growled, "The hell you will!"

Savage said, "We'll all go."

"Afraid I might run away? I can get away any time I really want to try."

"I wouldn't do it if I was you. From the looks of this trail, any one of us could follow it. Maybe we don't need you so much after all."

Bill Waymire said quickly, "You need him. The trail ain't always going to be like this."

Charlie shrugged and went on, with the others following close behind. He wasn't familiar with the country here and so didn't know who lived at the place ahead. Maybe, he thought hopefully, the smoke was coming from a barn the Indians had burned. Maybe it wasn't a house. Maybe there wouldn't be any more bodies to be buried, to stir up greater anger in the already angry whites.

A mile from the rising smoke, he crested a shallow rise and could see its source. It was not a barn that had been burned. It was a house. In the yard before it, there were several spots of white.

Clothing, perhaps. He couldn't tell as yet. He kicked his horse into a trot and the others came briskly on behind.

Bill was squinting. "I think I seen one of them white spots move."

"Clothes maybe, with the wind blowing them."

"There ain't no wind."

"Then maybe somebody's still alive." Charlie kicked his horse into a hard gallop, leaning forward, squinting against the glare. He saw the movement now himself, and he could tell it was a person. A woman, he thought. Probably naked the way the Indians had left her. She was damn lucky she wasn't dead.

They were still three hundred yards away when she looked up. She had been crawling toward something and now Charlie saw what it was. The remnants of her dress. She snatched up the rags and covered herself with them.

Charlie held back and let the others go ahead. After the experience she'd had, the sight of an Indian face, even an Indian dressed like a white, might send her into hysterics or worse. Bill stayed back with him, letting the sheriff take over. Savage rode to the woman and dismounted. She was weeping hysterically, completely unable to say anything coherently. Savage lifted her and put his arms around her. He held her, awkwardly and embarrassedly.

Charlie glanced around. A man lay behind the burned building, fully clothed, an arrow protruding from his back. The other white spots Charlie had seen were piles of flour the Indians had scattered around before setting fire to the house. Jimmy Welch looked back at them and asked, "What the hell are we goin' to do with *her?*"

Neither man replied. Charlie could hear Savage talking to her, his voice sympathetic and reassuring, but he couldn't make out anything Savage said. The woman looked to be about his own age. She was dirty, and her hair was a tangle, but her features were regular and he had an idea that when she was cleaned up she would probably look pretty nice. Her hair was dark and from what he'd seen before she covered herself, she was rounded the way a woman ought to be and not bony and thin the way so many ranch women were.

Savage released the woman and looked at Jimmy Welch. "Find something to dig with and start a grave."

Conger said impatiently, "To hell with that! We ain't got the time."

Savage said, "Get started."

Conger said, "No!"

Jimmy Welch looked uncertainly from one man to the other. Savage said, "We'll find your boy. An hour to be decent ain't going to make no difference." He was firm but it was plain he was trying not to offend Conger, who wielded a lot of influence in a community that elected Savage every two years.

Conger said, "No."

Savage looked straight at Jimmy Welch. "Get the shovel. Get going."

Conger opened his mouth to say something, then closed it without doing so. Jimmy hurried to the barn. He went in, emerging moments later with a shovel. He looked around uncertainly, then went up on a little rise behind the remains of the house and began to dig.

The woman, still trying awkwardly to cover herself, went into the barn. Savage gathered up several pieces of her clothing and carried them to the barn. He tossed then inside, calling, "Here's some more stuff, ma'am."

He returned to the others. Conger said, "What about her?"

"What about her?"

"I mean, what are we goin' to do with her?"

Savage said, "We can do either one of two things. We can send a man back to town with her, or we can take her along with us."

"We ain't got so many men that we can spare one for her."

"Then we take her along with us."

"The hell we do! She'll slow us down."

"Then we send a man with her to take her back to town."

Conger shook his head, staring at the open door of the barn.

Savage said, "Mr. Conger, I won't leave her here."

"You'll do what I tell you to!"

"No sir." Savage was embarrassed at having to clash with Conger, but he was adamant.

Conger's face got red. His eyes glittered. He stared at Savage for a moment. Savage stared back, his own face pale. At last Conger shrugged. "All right. We take her along. But first ranch or town we come to, we leave her off."

Savage nodded. "All right." He was visibly relieved. He started to explain his stand to Conger, then changed his mind. Conger knew and didn't have to be told. And if they found the boy, any animosity Conger might feel over this clash of wills would be forgotten quickly enough.

The woman came out of the barn. She was dressed now, though her clothes were badly torn. She had straightened her hair and had wiped the dirt from her face.

Charlie and Bill still sat their horses fifty feet away. She looked toward them and for a moment her eyes met Charlie's. A wild look came to them and she shrank away, half turning as if to run. Savage said quickly, "That's just Charlie Waymire, ma'am. He's an Indian, but he was raised like a white. Don't be afraid of him. He's helpin' us track down Mr. Conger's grandson them same Indians stole."

She nodded, still looking at Charlie fearfully. For the first time in his life, he was ashamed of being Indian.

Savage asked, "You see the boy with them?"

She nodded.

"Boy about five. Light hair."

She nodded again.

Conger broke in, "Ma'am, was he all right?"

She spoke for the first time. Her voice was shaken, but it had an oddly pleasant quality. "He was all right. His mouth was swelled up as if he had been hit and he was frightened, but he seemed to be all right."

Conger nodded, relief apparent in him. "When were they here?"

"Yesterday morning."

Savage said, "And you've been like this . . . all that time?"

She nodded, and raised a hand to her face, feeling the bruises there. "I was unconscious for a long time, I suppose. I came to every once in a while and then . . ." Her voice trailed off.

From the knoll, Jimmy called, "Hey, Sheriff! Is three feet deep enough?"

Conger answered for the sheriff. "Sure it is!"

Savage glanced at the woman, then at Conger. He hesitated, then called to Jimmy, "That's deep enough, I guess." Turning to Martinez and Tolliver he said, "Carry him up there."

The two crossed to the man's body. Tolliver broke the arrow off and tossed the piece aside. They picked the man up and carried him to the grave.

Savage said, "Ma'am, I ain't much good at this, but I'll say a few words over him if you want me to."

She glanced at him gratefully. "Would you?"

"Yes, ma'am."

Conger said impatiently, "Let's get at it."

The group walked up to the grave, Savage holding the woman's elbow. At the grave, he asked, "What was his name, ma'am?"

"John. John Roark."

"Yes, ma'am." Savage looked at Martinez and Tolliver. "Take off your hats."

They obeyed. Charlie and Bill, though they were a hundred feet away, also removed their hats. Savage said, "Lord, John Roark was a good man, cut down for no good reason by a bunch of murderin' redskins. I ask you to look kindly on him." He glanced across at Tolliver and Martinez and said, "Put him in. Carefully now, don't just dump him."

They picked up the body and lowered it as far into the grave as they could. They released it, then, and it dropped the last two feet with an audible thud. The woman winced. Savage said quickly, "Fill it in." He took the woman's arm. "Come on, ma'am. You figure you can ride?"

"I can ride." She did not look at the ruins of the house.

"Come on, then, I'll help you up." He helped her mount his own horse. He swung up behind her, settling himself on the horse's rump. He nodded at Charlie and Charlie led out, taking the Indians' trail again.

Back at the grave, Martinez and Tolliver worked at filling it. They'd catch up without difficulty.

Charlie didn't look back. Neither did the woman. The grim little procession crawled on west across the empty, dry brown land toward the high peaks they could not yet see.

Chapter 4

Behind him, Charlie could hear Joe Savage's sympathetic voice as he talked quietly with the woman in the saddle in front of him. "How long you lived here, ma'am?"

"A year, Mr. Savage."

"Call me Joe. Everybody does."

There was a short silence, and then she said, "My name is Edith. My husband called me Edie."

"Been married long?"

"A year. I met John in St. Louis."

"Like it out here, Mrs. Roark?"

She was silent for a moment. Charlie turned his head to glance at her and caught her looking at him. Her face was expressionless, yet he had the strange feeling that she was looking at the bruises on his face more than at the color of his skin. She glanced quickly away as his eyes met hers and said, "I don't know. I guess I did before the Indians came. I liked the solitude and the openness."

"Yes, ma'am. I like them things myself. You got family back there in St. Louis?"

"No. No family." She did not elaborate and Savage did not question her further.

Charlie knew what she must have endured while the Indians were here. She had been forced to witness the murder of her husband and the burning of her house. She had had the clothes ripped off her and had been raped repeatedly. A dark bruise beneath one eye and another on the other cheekbone, plus a smashed mouth, were proof that she had been beaten as well as raped. And the fact that she had slipped in and out of consciousness for a full twenty-four hours before they had found her testified to the awfulness of the experience.

Yet there must be a lot of strength in her or she wouldn't have been able to pull herself together as quickly

28

as she had. She wouldn't be able to ride today without
a lot of stubborn strength. Charlie found himself admir-
ing her enormously.

Apparently there had been some wind out here on the
previous day because the trail was beginning to blur in
the places where the wind had got a sweep at it.

As the morning progressed, they moved into broken
country. Now the land was cut by great, rocky ravines,
most of them dry in the bottom. Cedars and piñon pine
covered the slopes, and occasionally an escarpment of
rimrock raised itself above the level of the land.

On rocky ground, following the trail was more difficult. Charlie slowed his horse to a walk. Behind him,
Tolliver began to grumble about how slow he was. "He's
stallin'. He's holdin' us back so them murderin' savages
can get away."

Savage called, "Don't you try that, Charlie."

Anger flared in Charlie but he didn't look around. He
was a fool, he thought, thinking that if he helped them
find Danny Rutherford their attitudes would change. They
weren't ever going to change. At least not until twenty
or thirty years had passed. Still circulating were too many
stories of atrocity, both true and untrue, for them ever
to accept an Indian.

He heard Mrs. Roark's voice, even though she kept it
soft so that he wouldn't hear. "Why don't you trust him?"
she asked. "I thought you said he had been raised like
a white."

And Savage's reply, "He *has* been raised like a white,
ma'am, but he's still a red Indian underneath, an' you
can't trust none of 'em, no matter what."

"Isn't he helping you trail the Indians? Isn't he going
to help you get that boy back from them?"

"Sure he is, but it ain't by choice."

"Is that how he got the bruises on his face? Trying
to refuse?"

"Ma'am, just you never mind. After what's happened
to you, I wouldn't think you'd feel no sympathy for an
Indian."

Charlie felt his neck getting red, but he didn't turn
his head. Maybe he ought to be what they said he was,
a treacherous savage, trying to lead them into an ambush
or deliberately delaying them to give the party of young
braves time to get away.

Near noon, they came upon a buffalo hunters' camp. It lay on the bank of a wide, dry stream bed. Several wagons stood idle, their tongues resting on the ground. There was a rope corral with a few horses in it, and on the flat beyond the camp, dozens of buffalo hides were pegged out to dry.

Flies made a black cloud over the entire area, rising and buzzing as they were disturbed by the passage of the little cavalcade. Half a dozen wolves prowled among the drying hides, gray and glossy and fat, bold but not bold enough to come within rifle range. The strench was unbelievable.

Three hunters looked up from their fire, where they were cooking a big, bloody chunk of buffalo hump on a spit. They scowled at Charlie, who said nothing. They stared at Edie Roark, looking her up and down as if she were a saloon woman. With irritation in his voice, Savage said, "How long ago did that bunch of Indians pass by here?"

"Early yestiddy afternoon." The man grinned. "They didn't stop."

"Have a fight with them?"

"Couldn't rightly call it a fight. We burnt some powder an' they skeedaddled."

"Have a boy with them?"

" 'Twas one of 'em ridin' double, I recollect. White boy they takened, was he?"

Savage nodded. "Mr. Conger's grandson."

The hunter, bearded and dirty, with a cud of tobacco in his cheek, said, "Light, if ye're a mind. Hump will be ready in a spell."

Savage's expression said he couldn't possibly eat with a stench like this in his nose. He shook his head. "We'll go on. Thanks for the offer, anyway." He nodded at Charlie and Charlie rode on through the camp. Behind him, he heard the hunter ask, "Where'd ye pick up the redskin?"

Nobody bothered to answer him. He growled something about their being unsociable, and then Charlie passed out of hearing range.

Conger, Martinez and Tolliver stayed behind in the hunters' camp, talking to the three, though they did not dismount. The others were a quarter mile beyond the camp before they left it and came galloping to catch up. When they had, Savage turned his head. "What was that all about?"

"Askin' about the nearest ranch, or town," Conger replied. "So's we can get rid of *her*."

Savage said, "She ain't holdin' us back."

"The hell she ain't!"

Charlie Waymire turned his head. "She hasn't held us back so far. I'm following trail as fast as I can. It's not going to get any faster, either."

Tolliver growled, "Shut your mouth, redskin!"

Edith Roark turned her head and looked at him. Speaking to Savage, she asked, "What has he done? Why are you all so unpleasant to him?"

Charlie smiled faintly to himself. Savage grumbled, "He's an Indian. People can't help hatin' Indians after all that's happened out here. I'd think you could see that better than anybody else."

"*He* didn't have anything to do with what happened to me."

"No, ma'am, but they're all alike. Underneath that red hide they're all savages."

She didn't dispute what he said, probably, Charlie thought, because she could see it would be a waste of breath. Prejudices and hatreds, once formed, were hard to overcome. Grinning ruefully to himself, he thought that it would probably be as hard to persuade Indians to trust a white man as it was to persuade whites to trust an Indian.

Ahead, now, and faintly he could see clouds gathering over the invisible mountains. They'd drift east during the afternoon. It would rain. It might have rained yesterday up ahead. If it had, the trail would be all but obliterated.

But he didn't mention it to the others yet. They could see for themselves if and when they came to a place where it had rained.

They had gone no more than a couple of miles from the buffalo hunters' camp when Charlie heard the boom of a big bore buffalo gun off to his right. It boomed once, twice, then in regular cadence as quickly as it could be reloaded and fired again. Charlie thought, "He's got a stand."

He turned his head and looked at Bill. He switched his glance to Savage, who asked, "What do you think?"

Charlie said, "A stand. Likely that, anyhow."

"What else could it be?"

"Could be Indians. Fighting off Indians or shooting buffalo, the timing of the shots would be the same."

"Think we ought to take a look?"

Charlie shrugged. "Up to you. No matter what I said, I'd be accused of something." He knew if he said go on, they'd say he was trying to protect some attacking Indians. If he said investigate, he'd be accused of delaying them. Savage turned his head and glanced at Conger. "What do you want to do, Mr. Conger?"

"Look into it. It ain't very far out of our way and it could be the ones we're following."

Charlie immediately turned his horse toward the sound of the shots. They still boomed regularly. He didn't really think Indians were involved, but out here, you couldn't rule it out.

At a steady trot, the little group swept along. The shots continued, their cadence regular, their deep-throated boom unmistakable. A Sharps .50 caliber, Charlie thought, being fired from a rest.

They had traveled more than half the distance separating them from the source of the shots when Charlie heard another report. This one was sharper than that of the Sharps. He frowned slightly to himself.

It wasn't likely that the buffalo hunter would be using more than one kind of rifle. He probably wouldn't even possess more than one, and the report had not had the sharp bark of a pistol. It had been a rifle, unmistakably, but one of smaller bore than the hunter's Sharps.

He kicked his horse into a lope. Behind him, the others matched his pace. Savage called, "What the hell was that?"

Charlie replied superfluously, "Different gun. Rifle, but smaller bore."

"Meaning what?"

"Meaning the hunter's not alone."

"Then maybe it *is* Indians. That what you mean?"

Charlie grunted noncommittally. The land here was rolling, with low, rounded hills separating grassy parks. Ideal buffalo country, Charlie thought. Good grazing for them, and cover which would give them a feeling of security.

He galloped up over a long rise and pulled his horse

to a plunging halt at the top. Before him was a wider valley than those they had crossed previously. In the middle of it, twenty or thirty buffalo lay on the ground, a few still kicking or trying to raise their heads. The herd was running, a quarter mile away.

A faint smell of powdersmoke drifted to Charlie's nostrils on the breeze. He saw the hunter crouched behind some rocks on a slope above the dead and dying buffalo. On beyond, behind some other rocks at the crest of the slope, he saw the slender, bronzed upper body of an Indian, saw the glint of sun on the Indian's rifle barrel as he aimed and fired it.

Smoke puffed out from the muzzle. The report rolled along the slope. The hunter fired his own gun and Charlie saw its puff of bluish smoke, heard its booming report. As the hunter's bullet struck, dust puffed from the rock behind which the Indian had concealed himself. Before the hunter could reload, the Indian leaped quickly to his feet.

Carrying only a knife, he raced along the slope toward the hunter, who was busy reloading and did not glance up. Savage bawled, "Look out!"

The hunter looked up. The Indian was only a dozen yards away and coming fast. The hunter got to his feet, dropping his rifle. He snatched a revolver out of a holster hung from his belt.

He fired almost instantly. Hit, the Indian stumbled. He fell, sliding on the ground for several feet. Quickly he leaped up, veered down the slope to the doubtful cover of some scrubby brush. The hunter fired twice more, but missed both times.

Charlie and the others were already galloping down the slope. And suddenly Charlie saw something he hadn't seen before. A second Indian up behind the rocks where the first had been. This one now got up and ran along the slope toward the brush concealing the first. The second Indian was a squaw.

The hunter had gone back to reloading his rifle. Neither the wounded Indian nor his squaw were now armed. She had left his unloaded and therefore useless rifle in the rocks.

Charlie and the others reached the hunter. The man was maybe fifty, Charlie guessed, a thick-bodied man with a gray beard and gray hair that hadn't seen a barber's shears for more than a year. There was a stench to him like that in the buffalo hunters' camp, but here were other smells here, those of powdersmoke and sweat and of dead and dying buffalo less than a hundred yards away.

The squaw reached the concealment of the scrubby brush and flung herself down beside her man. The hunter grinned cheerfully, "Well now, I'm glad to see you folks. Not that I couldn't have handled it, you understand, but the red devil might have nicked me with a lucky shot."

Charlie said, "He'd have put a knife in you if Savage hadn't yelled."

"Would he now?" The man looked up at him. "Redskin yourself, ain't you?" He turned his glance to Savage again, noting the star on the sheriff's vest, noting Edith riding double with him. "What you folks doin' way out here?"

"Following some Indians. The ones that came though here yesterday."

"Oh yeah. Them." The hunter glanced at the brush behind which the Indians were hiding. "I'll have to dig those two out. They'll try gittin' me if I don't. Red devils think they own the buffalo. Don't think nobody else has got no rights at all."

Charlie said, "Maybe they don't think they ought to be wasted—slaughtered for their hides while Indians are hungry."

The hunter did not reply. Instead he looked at Savage. "Talks just like a real man now, don't he? Not like a stinkin' animal."

Tolliver said, "That squaw didn't look so bad. I'll help you dig 'em out." Charlie glanced at Tolliver's face. The man was sweating and his eyes were bright. Charlie looked at Conger. "We're wasting time."

Conger said, "Dig 'em out, Tolliver. Maybe one of 'em can tell us something about the bucks we're following."

Charlie felt an emptiness in his gut. Because what was coming wasn't going to be pleasant. And he couldn't stop it. Not unless he was willing to die beside the young Indian and his squaw.

Chapter 5

Tolliver rode cautiously toward the clump of scrubby brush behind which the Indians were hidden. The hunter accompanied him on foot, his big buffalo gun held ready in his hands. Welch and Martinez followed along behind the two. Conger and Savage stayed a ways behind.

Charlie glanced at Bill, who said softly, "Don't be a fool. Don't git yourself killed for nothin'."

"They're nothing?"

"That ain't what I meant and you know it ain't. But you can't change nothin' by givin' up your life."

The young Indian, seeing the white men approach, stood up. He had sheathed his knife and now stood facing them, arms folded, weaponless. The woman also stood up and took her place beside him, desperately afraid but trying to be as brave as he. Conger yelled at Charlie. "Ask him if he knows anything about the bunch that have Danny."

Charlie rode close. The four whites had formed a semicircle facing the two Indians. It was plain both the young brave and his squaw believed they were going to be killed. Charlie said haltingly in the Cheyenne tongue, "We are pursuing a party of Indians who have a white boy with them. Have you seen them?"

The brave glanced curiously at him, surprised to hear him speak Cheyenne. He shook his head.

Still speaking Cheyenne, Charlie said, "Why did you attack the hunter? Why did you do something so foolish?"

The Indian spoke. "He was killing the buffalo. He and others like him have killed many buffalo. It is now hard for us to find enough to eat."

Charlie couldn't look him in the eye. He wanted to explain why he wasn't going to help the two, but he knew how it would sound. He turned and looked at

Conger. He called, "They don't know anything about the ones we're following. Let them go."

The hunter roared, "Let 'em go? Are you crazy, redskin? They'll sneak up on us in the night an' murder us in our beds!"

Charlie looked at Savage. "Let them go," he called. "I can get them to agree to leave."

Savage glanced at Conger and Conger shook his head. He was staring at the two Indians, his eyes as cold as ice. What was in his mind was plain in his expression. He wanted vengeance against these two for the deaths of his daughter and her family.

Conger said, "Kill 'em."

The hunter turned his head. "Not the squaw. I'll take her. We been out here three goddam months, an' we ain't nowheres near ready to go back."

Conger said, "Kill 'em both."

Tolliver said, "Boss, let *me* have her. She can trail if that sonofabitch here quits on us."

Charlie saw how pale was Edith Roark's face. He felt an emptiness in his belly as he kneed his horse into position between the men and the two Indians. He said, "Let them be."

Tolliver swung his rifle until it pointed at Charlie's chest. "You shut up, redskin. You ain't got nothin' to say about anything."

Charlie glanced at Conger. "They didn't have anything to do with what happened to your daughter and her family."

Congar's voice was stubborn and cold. "Get out of the way."

The hunter's gun was up now and so was Tolliver's. The hunter looked around at Conger's face, hesitating.

Charlie said desperately, "You kill them and you've got to kill me too. Then who will trail for you?"

Conger hesitated. For the briefest instant, Charlie thought that he had won.

Edith Roark's face was ghastly as she stared at the Indians.

Suddenly then, almost beside Charlie and with a concussion that made his ears ring, Tolliver's rifle roared.

Charlie spurred his horse. The animal hit Tolliver's horse broadside and Charlie seized the rifle and twisted it out of the big man's hands. Reversing it, he struck

Tolliver on the ear with its butt and saw the man tumble from the saddle, to hit the ground like a sack of flour.

Ignoring the danger from the others, he glanced toward the two Indians. The brave was on the ground, his eyes staring at the sky. There was a spot of blood on his chest as big as the palm of a man's hand. He had been killed instantly.

For a moment, Charlie was too stunned to speak. Violence was no stranger to him. He had lived through two attacks by soldiers upon the villages where he and his family lived.

But this was the most deliberate, cold-blooded act of murder he had ever seen. He glared furiously at the mounted men, then at the hunter on the ground. He raged, "God damn you all to hell!"

Bill yelled, "Charlie! Shut up!" Bill was aware, if Charlie was not, how contagious murder is. Charlie himself was no more than a hair's breadth from death. Guns were pointed at him, fingers curled on triggers, but Charlie didn't seem to care.

The hunter raised his gun. Edith Roark screamed, "Stop it! Stop!" Conger's voice cut the silence like a whip. "Put that damn thing down!"

The hunter turned his head. "Who the hell are you to tell me what to do, old man?"

Conger said icily, "I've got four men with me who will back up what I say."

The hunter lowered his gun. Scowling he said, "I don't give a damn how many you got with you, I'm takin' that squaw with me!"

The squaw was on the ground beside her man, weeping, wailing the way Indian women do.

Conger said, "Take her then. I don't care."

Tolliver was stirring. He struggled to his hands and knees and peered painfully up at Charlie and at the others just beyond. He switched his glance to the woman, then pushed himself unsteadily to his feet. Conger let a faint, malicious smile play across his mouth. "The hunter wants her too, Bart. Looks like it's between the two of you."

Tolliver swung his massive head and glared at the hunter. He said thickly, "She's mine."

Conger teased, "Settle it between yourselves."

Charlie glanced at him. Conger was tough and old

and possessed of a cold dignity. This was a side of him
Charlie had not seen before. He was deliberately pitting
these two men against each other just for the fun of it.
He was jeopardizing his pursuit of the Indians who had
his grandson just to see a fight to the death between two
men, one of whom was his foreman and, because he was
hurt, likely to lose his life.

Savage growled, "Forget it! Get on your horse, Tolliver. We're getting out of here."

Tolliver swung his head. "The hell! I want that little
squaw."

He swung to face the hunter, but the hunter didn't
wait for him. He rushed, rifle held across his chest,
and when he reached Tolliver, he brought it viciously
upward, catching Tolliver under the chin with the re-
ceiver.

The hammer gashed his throat and the blood spurted
out. His head slammed back and the force of the hunter's
body, striking him immediately afterward, knocked him
off his feet.

The fight was over scarcely before it had begun. Conger said sourly, "Load the sonofabitch on his horse so
we can go."

The hunter stood looking down at Tolliver. Tolliver's
blood was on his hands. He still held the rifle across his
chest and now he swung his head to stare at the squaw.

She was on her knees, her head buried in her husband's
chest. Her hair, black as night, lay in gleaming folds
over the young brave's face. The hunter moved toward
her.

Standing over her, he said, "Come on. You got yourself a new man now."

She did not look up. The hunter turned his head.
"Tell her," he said to Charlie.

Charlie said wearily, "Tell her yourself."

The hunter leaned over the squaw. Putting down his
rifle he slid his hands under her arms from the rear,
letting them slide forward and cup themselves over her
breasts. "I ain't gonna hurt you, woman. You come with
me an' we'll get along just fine." He lifted her bodily.

Charlie opened his mouth to yell a warning, but he
was too late. Something flashed in the sunlight, the knife
that the squaw had snatched from the sheath at the
dead brave's waist.

All any of them could do was watch. The squaw was young, and strong, and quick. She pulled free, whirled and buried the knife in the hunter's bulging paunch. As quickly, she withdrew it and plunged it in again, her face twisted with grief and shock.

The hunter staggered back, both hands clutching his belly. Blood leaked through his fingers and he stared down at it unbelievingly as if he couldn't comprehend what was happening. He looked up at Charlie, and beyond at the others, and then he suddenly sat down on the ground.

The squaw stood facing them, the dripping knife in her hand. Conger raised his gun deliberately, sighting it on her as if she had been a coyote or a wolf.

Charlie spurred his horse. The animal leaped forward. Conger's gun cracked and the animal reared, burned across the chest by the bullet that, undeflected, went on to strike the squaw in the chest.

Charlie was busy fighting his plunging, terrified horse, but he saw her collapse. She fell a few feet away from the dead Indian brave. Still living, but barely so, she struggled and crawled, until she could touch his face with her hand.

She died then, quietly, without making a sound, her hand resting on the dead brave's face. Edith Roark suddenly began to weep.

Savage said protestingly, "You didn't have to kill her!"

Sarcastically Conger said, "What would *you* do with her? Take her back to town and put her on trial for murdering that hunter there?"

Charlie now had his horse under control, but he was rapidly losing control of himself. He reached for his rifle, but a strong, thick-fingered hand gripped his wrist and kept him from withdrawing it. Bill's voice said, "Whoa! Your dyin' ain't goin' to help them two."

Charlie couldn't speak. The blood was pounding in his head. He could feel the sweat springing out all over his face. Never before in his life had he wanted so much to kill. Martinez's voice came, thick with an accent that wasn't noticeable unless he was upset. "Let him go, Waymire. Let's kill all the red devils right now and get it over with."

Conger said, "No!" He looked at Charlie. "Get back to that trail."

Charlie looked him straight in the eye. "You go to hell!"

Conger gave him a small, frosty smile. "You know the alternative, don't you?"

Charlie looked at the bodies on the ground. He shrugged fatalistically. "What about them?"

Conger said, "Martinez, you and Welch load that hunter on his horse. Take him back to his camp and tell his friends there are twenty or thirty buffalo out here waiting to be skinned."

Charlie asked, "What about the Indians?"

There was sarcasm in Conger's voice. "What do you think we ought to do with them? Take them to their sacred burial ground?"

Charlie said, "You could bury them. If you leave them here the wolves will work on them."

Conger said, "We're looking for my grandson, remember?"

"What if I just plain refuse to help?"

"We'll kill you and leave you here with *them*."

"You don't sound much like you did back there at the Rutherford place."

"Maybe not, but that was back at the Rutherford place. Way it turned out, we didn't need you to follow trail. Any one of us could have followed it."

Charlie shrugged. Martinez and Welch already had the dead hunter on his horse. They tied him down with his own rope. Both men mounted and, with Welch leading the horse, they headed back toward the hunters' camp.

Charlie rode back toward the place where they had left the trail. He felt dirty and ashamed, as if he had helped kill the two Indians himself.

Edith Roark continued to sob hysterically. Savage tried to comfort her, but she would not be comforted. The violence she had just witnessed had, in her condition, simply been more than she could stand. Charlie realized that he hated these five white men more than he would have thought possible yesterday. For the first time he considered leading them into a trap. It was only what they deserved.

Chapter 6

Though Charlie's anger smoldered dangerously, there was something else in his mind that was even worse. It was a dull feeling of hopelessness over the brutality of what had happened at the buffalo hunter's stand. Two young Indians lay dead whose only wrongdoing, if it could be called that, had been that they objected to the slaughter of buffalo for their hides. They had been murdered callously, with the sheriff looking on and giving the whole thing the blessing of the white man's law.

He felt Bill's glance and turned his head. The old man's eyes mirrored his own outrage, but behind that outrage, pain was visible. Bill said softly, "We couldn't have changed anything. If we'd tried, we'd be layin' back there with them two Indians."

"Why couldn't we have changed anything?"

"Because Conger an' Tolliver an' Martinez was bent on murder. All they was lookin' for was the victims."

"The sheriff let them do it. Is that what the law is all about?"

"The law is men, Charlie. It's made by men an' enforced by men. It ain't no more perfect than the men theirselves."

Charlie only scowled.

Bill said, "What about the law in the Indian villages, Charlie?"

"They have laws," Charlie said defensively.

"Sure. But do their laws keep 'em from stealin' horses from an enemy? Do they keep 'em from raidin', like they did back there at Rutherfords' an' Roarks'?"

"That's different."

"Is it? You think killin' Roark was any better than killin' them two Indians? You think them eight bucks

41

rapin' Mrs. Roark was any better'n what Tolliver an' the hunter had in mind for that Indian squaw?"

Charlie said, "Damn you, don't take my mad away from me."

"I ain't tryin' to," growled Bill, and let it drop.

All afternoon they rode steadily west. The trail faded and disappeared as they passed across an area where a cloudburst had struck the day before. Five miles farther, on, where the storm had missed, Charlie quartered back and forth like a hound. After a wasted hour and a half he found the trail again, faint because a light rain had fallen even here, but plain enough to follow at a walk.

Near sundown, Conger said, "The hunters said an old bachelor lived half a dozen miles north of that elephant-shaped butte. We can leave the woman there."

Savage nodded reluctantly. The old goat, Charlie thought. He likes having her sitting there close to him, and he felt a touch of anger at the idea of Savage putting his hands on her.

Afterward, he puzzled at himself, wondering why he cared. She was nothing to him and would never be. There was a gulf between them as wide as the Rocky Mountains, a gulf that couldn't be bridged even if either of them wanted to bridge it, which they did not. He put his attention on the new direction they were traveling, absently marking the place where they had left the trail in his mind so that it could be quickly picked up again the next day. They passed by the grayish sandstone butte on the eastern side, dwarfed by its enormous size.

It was nearly dark when, following a small stream bed, the bottom of which was damp from yesterday's rain and showed signs of the flood it had carried the day before, they reached the bachelor's small shack.

It was a two-room affair, half of it built of boards, the other half of sod. The roof was sod, with weeds and grass three feet high growing out of it.

A man came to the door, barefooted, wearing pants but no shirt. He had on dirty red-flannel underwear. There was a small corral containing a single horse near the shack, and there was a wagon, its tongue resting on the ground.

Charlie lagged, letting Savage and Conger take the lead. He dropped all the way back to the party's rear and halted his horse, wanting nothing to do with negotiations concerning the fate of Mrs. Roark.

But he could hear the talk. Savage said, "Howdy," and the man in the doorway scratched his belly, rubbed the whiskers on his face and nodded in reply.

Savage said. "This here is Mrs. Roark. Her place was burned out and her man killed a couple of days ago."

Still the man in the doorway didn't speak. His eyes were on Edith Roark, steady and unblinking enough to make her look uncomfortably away. Savage said, "I'd like you to take her in to town where she'll be safe."

"What town?" The man's voice was harsh and raspy as if he didn't use it much, which indeed he probably did not.

"Nearest one. Which is that?"

"Pueblo's the nearest town. Fort Lyon's closer. Mebbe a hunerd an' twenny mile."

"You can take her there."

"Why should I? What's in it for me?"

Savage looked at Conger helplessly. Conger said, "Twenty dollars."

"Gold?"

"Gold." Conger fished in his pocket, found a twenty-dollar gold piece and tossed it to the man, who caught it expertly.

Savage said, "Long's we're here, we'd just as well spend the night."

Conger nodded. Savage said, "Picket your horses where there's grass. Water 'em first over there where the gulch is dug out."

The men dismounted. Charlie and Bill waited until they had all watered their horses, then watered their own. Charlie took both horses then and led them out far enough so that there would be plenty of grass for them. He picketed them and returned, still brooding about what had happened at noon.

Smoke now rose from the chimney of the shack. Members of the posse had built fires of their own out in the yard, using buffalo chips from the huge pile in the squatter's yard. There also was an ill-smelling pile of bleaching bones, nearly as large as the shack itself. It was about an eighth of a mile away, and only occasionally did the breeze bring the smell of it into the squatter's yard.

Bill had built a small fire for Charlie and himself, as

far away from the others as he could. He had coffee on. Charlie hunkered down and stared moodily into the almost smokeless flames. Without looking up, he asked, "Where's it going to end?"

Bill did not immediately answer that. Charlie glanced up at him. Bill said, "Hell, boy, I don't know. If you think they're goin' to like you, even if you help 'em find the kid, then you're barkin' up the wrong tree. Best you can hope for is to stay alive, I'd say. That's the best either of us can hope for. That an' the chance to go on back home again."

"Then why did we come?"

Bill grinned ruefully. "We came because we didn't have no choice."

"They wouldn't have killed us. Not back there."

"Wouldn't they? I ain't so sure of that."

"Then we've got everything to lose and nothing to gain."

"That's about the size of it."

Charlie said with bitter humor, "No wonder us redskins hate the damn white man."

"Hatin' the white man ain't goin' to get you nowhere." The coffee boiled and Bill picked up the pot. He poured Charlie a cup and one for himself, then put some bacon on to fry. He said, "The white man's here to stay."

Charlie sipped the coffee. He had been born an Indian at the wrong time in history, he thought. Fifty years ago, there had been no white men here. Fifty years from now, red men and white would have learned to live in peace.

He took the plate of food that Bill handed him and sat down cross-legged on the ground to eat. It was dark now, and the fire highlighted the planes of his face and his hawklike nose. Indian, he was, but he did not have the broad features that many Indians had.

The man came out of his shack carrying a pail and went to the waterhole in the dry stream bed. He filled his pail with water and shuffled back toward the house. He stared at Edith Roark until he had passed her and no longer could. Charlie asked, "What's his name? I never heard him say."

"I guess nobody asked him. I guess nobody cares."

"All they want to do is get rid of her. They don't give a damn what happens to her afterward."

Bill peered at him. "Do you?"

"Sure I do. She's had a bad time of it."

"She probably hates Indians worse than any of them."

"I doubt that. Maybe she hates the eight that killed her husband and burned them out, but she don't hate every Indian."

Bill got his blankets. "I'm going to turn in."

Charlie nodded and got his own blanket roll. He lay down close to the fire, which now had died to a bed of grayish coals.

For a long time, he stared up at the sky. It was partly overcast, but stars shone through here and there. Across the fire, Bill began to snore.

Most of the others also had turned in. The window of the shack was dark. Its occupant was a surly and unsavory bastard, Charlie thought. He hadn't spoken to anybody after that first exchange with Conger when they arrived. But he'd stared at Edith Roark every chance he got. He'd probably been staring at her through the dirty window of his shack whenever he was inside.

Charlie felt guilty about leaving her, yet he knew he had nothing to do with it. He had nothing to say, one way or another.

She was a strong and capable woman, he thought. She could take care of herself. Or could she? The occupant of this squatter's shack, however unsavory, had twice her strength.

He closed his eyes. Forget it, he told himself. It's none of your concern.

He slept lightly, the way he almost always did. A scream awakened him and he sat straight up, throwing his blankets off. He reached for the rifle at his side.

He heard it again, and this time was able to identify it. It was a woman's cry and it came from the place where Edith Roark had made her bed.

He leaped to his feet. Barefooted, he crossed the yard in the darkness at a run, avoiding the rising shapes of men aroused by the woman's cries. He could hear Bill stumbling along behind him. He heard him collide with someone and heard both of them curse.

Edith Roark's attacker could only be one of two. The occupant of this shabby squatter's shack. Or Tolliver, who had so badly wanted the Indian squaw.

It was dark, but there was some light coming from

the stars.. In this faint glow he could see two shapes struggling on the ground ahead of him. Edith Roark had stopped screaming. Now she was fighting, desperately, silently, and the only sounds she made were those of exertion.

Her attacker was also making sounds of exertion, deep, grunting, almost animal-like sounds. Charlie felt sudden fury. Bad enough that she had seen her home destroyed and her husband killed. Bad enough that she had been brutally beaten and raped by the eight Indians who had attacked their ranch. But now she was under attack by a man of her own race, and that was worse.

He reached the two. Even in the poor light it was easy to distinguish between the two struggling forms. Charlie had his rifle and he struck the man on the side of the head with its barrel. He was rewarded by a surprised, high yell of pain.

He could have struck again. He could have knocked the man unconscious. But he suddenly wanted more than that.

He'd been beaten himself by Martinez and Tolliver. He'd been humiliated, forced into coming along against his will. He'd been treated with contempt.

This man offered him release. Reaching down, he seized the man and yanked him away from Edith Roark. He said in a soft and savage voice, "Get up, you sonofabitch!"

The man had an unpleasant, sour smell. He staggered away, turned and faced Charlie, half crouching, wearing only his dirty red-flannel underwear.

Behind him, Charlie heard Conger's voice, "What the hell's going on?"

And Bill's voice in reply, "Stay out of it."

The squatter rushed. Charlie was ready, and stepped nimbly to the side, avoiding the man's clumsy rush. This would be easy, he thought, as his fist lashed out, landing on the man's ear and sending him tumbling to the ground.

Charlie's hand felt like it was broken, but he didn't care. There had been fierce pleasure in the contact. He stepped toward the man, waiting for him to rise and turn and come on again. When he did, Charlie landed a vicious blow on his mouth and felt lips and teeth give before the blow. The man stayed on his knees for almost a minute this time before he got up again. When he did,

Charlie got his nose and it burst like a ripe plum, sending the man to his knees again.

Conger said, "That's enough!" But it wasn't enough for Charlie. Knowing he was going to be stopped, he stepped close to the squatter and, as he got up, raised his knee into the man's face.

He caught him on the point of the chin and the man fell back, to lie spread-eagled and unconscious on the ground.

Savage asked, "You hurt, ma'am?"

She was weeping now. Between sobs, she said, "I guess not."

Savage said, "Conger, we can't leave her here."

"Why not? She can take care of herself. Even if she can't, nothin's goin' to happen to her that hasn't happened plenty of times before."

Savage said, "I'm not going to leave her here. He'll make a slave out of her. He won't take her to town until he's tired of her, if he does it then."

Conger said, "I'm not taking her any further."

"And I'm not leaving her."

Charlie said, "Neither am I."

"Shut up," said Conger. He turned to the sheriff again. "I'll remind you that you can't get reelected without my support."

Savage said, "I've heard that just about enough. If I don't get reelected, there are other jobs."

There was a long silence after that. Charlie grinned in the darkness, pleased at the stubbornness with which Savage had stood his ground. At last Conger said, "God damn it, how the hell are we ever going to catch up with them Indians, draggin' her along?"

Neither Savage nor Charlie replied to that. Savage went into the shack and brought the pail outside. It was still half full and he trickled it straight down into the unconscious man's face. When the man sat up, gasping, Savage said, "Get in that house and don't come out again until we're gone. Try anything like shooting one of us and your bones will bleach out here."

The squatter shuffled toward the shack. Savage asked, "You all right now, Mrs. Roark?"

"I guess I am."

"I'll leave my deputy on guard the rest of the night. Good night, ma'am."

"Good night, Sheriff."

She turned her head, trying to see Charlie's face. "Thank you, Mr. Waymire."

It was the first time anybody had ever called him that. He didn't know what to say. So instead of answering, he turned and stalked away.

From the darkness he heard Conger mutter, "The dumb sonofabitch! If he'd waited another few hours, he could have done anything he wanted to with her."

He hated Conger for that remark. More than he had hated any of the others for the things they had done to him.

Chapter 7

In the morning, the squatter did not even emerge from his shack as they made preparations to leave, and no smoke rose from the chimney.

But when Charlie glanced back, from a quarter mile away, he saw the man, still in his underwear, standing in front of the door, staring after them in the gray morning chill.

The sun came up. An hour after leaving the squatter's shack, they struck the trail again and Charlie turned into it.

For three hours, he maintained a steady trot. He slowed then, and traveled at a walk for a couple more. They halted briefly at noon, and went on afterward, with Charlie now warily watching the puffy white thunderheads building in the west.

As the afternoon progressed, the thunderheads rolled east. Bill grunted, "Looks like we're goin' to have a rain."

Charlie nodded. "Heavy one. One that could wash out the trail."

"It better not. You're in trouble if it does. Conger's as mad as a teased rattlesnake."

But the thunderheads continued to build to towering proportions that promised heavy rain and probably hail as well. They turned from white to gray, blotted out the sun, and darkened even more until it was as if dusk lay upon the land. At four, the first big drop struck Charlie's face. He turned and looked at Conger. The man was getting a poncho from behind his saddle. The others, those who had them, also got their ponchos out. Neither Charlie nor Bill had thought to bring one along. Savage gave his to Edith Roark. Charlie just pulled the brim of his hat farther down.

More huge raindrops fell, kicking up spurts of dust where they struck the ground. And now, ahead, Charlie could see a thick gray curtain marching toward them, beyond which nothing was visible.

It was going to be heavy, all right, he thought. Heavy enough to completely wipe out the trail they were following. He turned up the collar of his coat and ducked his head. He rode straight toward the curtain of rain, now less than a quarter mile away.

It struck with a fury that drenched him to the skin in less than a minute. It poured in a stream off the front of his hat brim. It turned the ground to a sea of mud in minutes and, as he had feared, completely and finally wiped out the trail.

Charlie didn't say anything because there wasn't any use, and besides, in the roar of the storm, it was doubtful if he could have made himself heard. Lightning bolts snaked out of the sky, one striking the ground so close that Charlie's horse reared with fright. Thunder crashed, its echoes rolling back and forth across the streaming land.

The rain turned to hail, pellets the size of marbles, and they beat down upon the riders mercilessly. The horses laid back their ears. The men simply ducked their heads, turning their faces away from the drive of it.

The ground turned white as the hail accumulated. It made the earth-brown rivers of water white. Where it wasn't washed away, hail was two inches deep in a few minutes, and still it came.

Behind him, his voice seeming faint over the roar of the storm, Conger bawled, "Have you lost the trail?"

It was a stupid question, one that Charlie didn't bother to answer. Anyone could see that there could be no trail with two inches of hail lying on the ground. Conger roared again, "Injun!"

Charlie turned his head.

"Have you lost the trail?"

Charlie nodded.

"Then we might as well stop!"

Savage bawled, "What for? There's no shelter!"

Conger roared, "Redskin, if you see any shelter, head for it!"

Charlie ducked his head and went on. The storm showed no sign of diminishing, even though by now the sky was lighter in the west.

Looming suddenly out of the gloom ahead, he saw a

rising sandstone bluff. It was only a quarter mile away. He kicked his horse into a trot.

The horse also saw the bluff and headed for it eagerly. The others came along behind, their mounts slipping and sliding in the muck underfoot.

Charlie reached the bluff. Here, suddenly, it was still. The wind howled overhead, but it was quiet in the lee of the bluff.

Charlie swung to the ground. It had hailed here too, but less, perhaps because the wind carried the rain and hail on beyond this sheltered place.

Cedars and a few stunted pines grew close against the bluff. In crevices on up the face of rock, others clung. Charlie was shivering from the cold. Bill said, "Let's get some wood. Maybe we can find some that will be dry."

Charlie thought of how good a fire would feel. He nodded and went looking for wood, careful not to go too far, careful to stay in view of those in camp. They had attacked him before when he headed away from camp to search for wood and he would as soon that didn't happen to him again.

Savage dismounted and helped Edith Roark to alight. He tied his horse to a stunted tree.

Under an overhang, Charlie found an armload of wood that was powder dry. He made a fire against the face of rock and the others came crowding close, trying to get warm. Bill brought a big armload of wet wood and spread it between the blaze and the rock face to dry.

Standing there close to the fire, Charlie's clothes began to steam. Edith Roark looked at him and gave a small, wan smile. Savage saw the smile and frowned. Charlie felt a touch of irritation. He didn't want Edith Roark and she certainly did not want him. But Savage acted as if . . . He made a disgusted grunt. Butting his head against white prejudice was about as useful as banging it against the sheer rock face of the bluff. He stared into the flames, turning around occasionally so that his back would get dry too.

The sky grew lighter as the clouds drove east. The rain diminished and finally it stopped. But there was a cold chill in the air from all the hail accumulated on the ground. Charlie could see his breath.

Conger said, "Think you can pick up the trail farther on?"

"I can try."

"That storm wasn't general. A few miles from here it's probably dry."

Charlie didn't believe that, but he didn't dispute Conger's word. He'd found the trail after losing it once before. Perhaps he could do so again. If he couldn't, he was in trouble and so was Bill. Not a man in the posse had any use for him. Several hated him bitterly enough to want him dead. If he lost the trail, they'd turn their thirst for vengeance against him. In the absence of guilty Indians, they'd punish him.

Savage said, "We'd just as well stay here for the night."

Surprisingly, Conger agreed. He was probably too wet and cold and tired to want to go on tonight. Quite possibly he recognized the futility of it. Tomorrow the hail would have melted and the ground would be firm again. They would make better time.

The others went searching for dry wood and started a couple more fires against the sheer rock face. They gathered wet wood and put it nearby to dry.

Bill made coffee and fried the last of the bacon. In the grease, he fried the last of the biscuits he had brought along. He grunted, "Have to find some grub tomorrow. Maybe we can kill a deer or buffalo."

Charlie asked softly, "What the hell are we goin' to do?"

"Do?"

"I'll never find that trail tomorrow. This rain washed it out for twenty miles. I'll be lucky if I ever find it again."

Bill said, "Don't tell *them* that."

Charlie grinned. "I hadn't planned to. But they'll find it out soon enough. And when they do . . ."

"If you can get away tonight, you'd better do it."

"What about you?"

"I'll stay."

"And what will I do? The Indians wouldn't take me back."

"Go to Denver. I'll sell the ranch and meet you there. We can go to Texas or someplace and buy another one."

Charlie nodded. His throat felt tight and he couldn't look at Bill.

As soon as everyone had finished eating they placed their beds close against the rock face where it was dry.

Conger said, "Tolliver, you stand guard until midnight. Martinez can take it until dawn."

"You think the redskin will try to get away?"

"He'll try."

Charlie glanced at Bill. "So much for that idea."

Bill grunted agreement. Both he and Charlie lay down near the face of the bluff, one on either side of the fire. Charlie closed his eyes. He knew Bill was awake and he knew Bill would probably stay awake, watching to see if either Tolliver or Martinez dozed off. It wasn't likely, but it was a chance.

He found it difficult to go to sleep himself. He couldn't see any chance of picking up the Indians' trail again unless it would be by some incredible of luck. The storm had been heavy and he was willing to bet it had been general. It had covered a swath fifteen or twenty miles wide and at least that long.

He slept, finally, but it was an uneasy sleep. He awakened often. Once he saw Bill up, renewing the fire. At midnight he heard Martinez take over the sentry duty from Tolliver.

The sky was gray when he next awoke. Bill was up, rebuilding the fire. Charlie rolled out, put on his boots and crowded close to the fire trying to get warm. There was a heavy frost on the ground. There was a crust of ice on the puddles that still remained.

Nobody had any food this morning. Charlie satisfied himself with a cup of coffee. He saddled his horse, filled his canteen from a rivulet coming out of a crevice in the rock, and waited until the others would be ready to go. He still had his rifle, which was loaded. He still had his revolver but that was in his saddlebags and he didn't want to attract attention by getting it out. Bill was also armed.

The sun came out as they pulled out of camp. Charlie elected to go south and try to get around the bluff, because it looked more promising. He led and the others followed. Bill fooled around in camp long enough so that, when he did ride out, he brought up the rear. It was a maneuver whose significance was not lost on Charlie. With luck, Bill would be able to get the drop on the others when the time for the showdown came.

It took an hour to find a way up over the bluff. It was a narrow trail, and Charlie studied it with care. The rain had done its work. This trail, which was in a narrow gulch, had carried a rivulet of water down off the top of the bluff. Vegetation had been beaten down by hail. Charlie could find no sign that anyone or anything had ever passed this way.

The sun on his back made his clothes, still damp from the day before, steam in the morning chill. But the warmth went through and he began to feel a little more cheerful than he had earlier. Maybe Conger and Tolliver and Martinez wouldn't try to kill him if he couldn't find the trail again. Maybe they'd figure they still needed him. He stared ahead toward the distant horizon, trying to guess which way the Indians might have gone.

There must be several villages within twenty or thirty miles. They were getting close to the Republican River. The village the renegades were headed for was probably on the Republican. But where? And even if they found it, how would they find the renegades?

The morning dragged. At noon, they stopped to rest the horses and let them eat a little grass. The rain had been as heavy here as it had been farther east. All trails, even those of animals, were gone.

After half an hour's rest, Charlie led out again. Bill stayed in the rear. Edith Roark, sensing something, was beginning to look scared. Conger, Tolliver and Martinez wore scowls of frustration. Conger's eyes had a look to them that was almost desperate.

And in Charlie there was also something desperate. If he didn't find the trail by nightfall, he was in trouble. Bad trouble, worse than any he had ever known before.

Chapter 8

Charlie was conscious, all through the afternoon, of their angry stares. He seemed to feel them boring into his back, but he did not look around for fear that doing so might precipitate what he knew was coming eventually anyway.

Desperately, he quartered back and forth, hoping to pick up the trail. He found nothing but the trail of three buffalo, made after the rain had stopped.

At dusk, he knew there was no longer any use. He stopped, turned his head and looked Conger squarely in the face. "It's no use, Mr. Conger. The rain must have covered a swath fifty miles long. The trail's gone and I haven't been able to find it again."

Tolliver growled, "Or you don't want to find it again."

With surprising self-control, Conger said, "We'll camp here for the night."

Savage slid from his saddle, then turned and helped Edith Roark alight. She was stiff from riding and as she started away, she stumbled and nearly fell. Savage watched her in a way that made Charlie smile faintly to himself. Savage was smitten, despite the fact that he was twice her age. It was surprising what proximity to an attractive woman would do to a man, even a crusty old bachelor like Savage.

Bill watched the proceedings carefully from his saddle, his hand on his rifle stock. When nothing happened, he dismounted stiffly and led his horse away. Unseen by either Charlie or Bill, Conger nodded at Tolliver, and the burly foreman followed Bill, also leading his horse.

Now Conger faced Charlie, who had dismounted and had started to lead his horse away. "You didn't try to find that trail today. You wanted them murderers to get away!"

Charlie glanced around. He let his glance go past

55

Conger to Martinez, who stood just behind him. The faces of both were grim and determined. Charlie protested, "That ain't true, Mr. Conger. I did my best. Nobody could have done any more."

"You callin' me a liar, boy?"

"No." A familiar tension had come to Charlie's arms and legs. His belly felt empty and cold. He looked beyond Conger and Martinez in the direction Bill had gone. Bill was a hundred yards away, with Tolliver between him and the camp.

Bill was headed toward a little draw, where a number of willows and cottonwoods grew, probably intending to water his horse and fill his canteen. He would get no help from Bill, he thought. He was on his own. Nor would the sheriff or his deputy interfere.

Desperately he said, "Tomorrow. I'll find it tomorrow."

"Not you." Conger turned his head. "Take him."

Martinez moved forward, his rifle at the ready in both hands. Charlie lunged for his own rifle in the saddle boot. Startled, his horse swung away and Charlie's hand missed the rifle stock.

Martinez now was close. He jabbed the rifle muzzle into Charlie's midsection, driving an explosive gust of air from him.

Pain knifed through Charlie's belly, doubling him, making him gasp involuntarily. Martinez clipped him on the ear with the rifle barrel. Charlie fell to his knees, still holding onto his horse's reins.

The horse danced away. Charlie used the pull to help him to his feet, but he couldn't straighten up. From the direction Bill had gone, he heard a yell, "Hey! Cut that out!"

Bill would try to help, but Tolliver would see that he did not. He looked for Martinez, caught movement to one side and swung his head that way. He was in time to get Martinez's rifle butt squarely in the mouth. It smashed his lips and probably knocked loose some teeth, he thought, as he released the reins and lunged for his saddle a second time, once more trying to seize his rifle and withdraw it from the boot.

Conger put a bullet into the ground between him and the horse and Charlie stopped as if he had run into a wall. His whole face was numb from the blow of the Mexican's rifle butt. His chest and belly ached ferociously so that it was difficult to stand upright. Bill was immobilized, and he was unarmed and he knew, with sick certainty, what they were going to do. They were going to kill him, here and now, in this desolate, lonely place. They were going to leave him lying just as they had left the young Indian and his squaw lying unburied back near the buffalo hunters' camp. If Bill fought to save him, they'd leave Bill lying dead beside him, and they'd go on, or they'd go back, and not one of them would feel the slightest remorse over the murder they had done.

Conger's voice came through the haze of pain, as clear and sharp as the tolling of a bell. "Hang him," Conger said harshly. And that was all, except for a gasp of protest from Edith Roark.

Savage said, "Ma'am, you stay out of this."

"Stay out of it?" she protested in disbelief. "He's a man, even if his skin *is* red. He's committed no crime and he's not been brought before any court of law."

Conger growled, "You can't bring an Injun into court, ma'am. They ain't subject to the laws we are. Indian Bureau takes care of 'em, an' mostly they get away with what they've done."

"But he's done nothing!"

"Stay out of it, Mrs. Roark, or I'll just have you taken away until it's over with."

"Do you mean to say you're really going to hang that man?"

Conger didn't answer her. He said, "Bring him, an' bring his horse. There's a tree big enough down there."

Edith Roark said despairingly, "Sheriff, for the love of God . . ."

"Stay out of it, ma'am. This ain't a thing a woman would understand."

Martinez prodded Charlie brutally in the back with his rifle muzzle. Charlie started to walk in the direction Conger had indicated, knowing Martinez would hit him again with the rifle barrel if he did not. He stumbled and almost fell, but quickly recovered himself. He did not look at Edith Roark.

Bill stood watching, a look of disbelief on his face. The sky was now deep gray, and in this cold light there was an unreality about the scene. There ought to be bonfires and torches at a hanging, Charlie thought, suppressing a desire to laugh hysterically.

He was going to die. He was actually going to die, and there was nothing either he or Bill could do. He gathered his muscles, preparatory to breaking free and running, then stopped himself. He wasn't dead until the rope snapped tight. Until then there was a~chance— that Savage would intervene—that Bill would somehow get hold of his gun and put a stop to it. If he ran, they'd either kill him with a bullet or they'd knock him out with a rifle barrel against the head. And then it really would be too late.

He stumbled toward the draw. One cottonwood towered above the rest, and it had a branch that was horizontal enough to support a hangman's rope. As he passed Bill, he glanced at him fleetingly. Bill roared, "No! No, by God!" and lunged for his horse where his rifle was.

They should never have let their guns get out of reach, Charlie thought, as Martinez put a bullet into the ground a step in front of Bill. Bill stopped, swinging his head toward the Mexican who said, "Go ahead, you Indian-lovin' sonofabitch! Go ahead, an' give me an excuse."

Bill stood frozen, looking at Charlie, trying to tell him with his glance that this wasn't over yet. Martinez said, "Go on, redskin. Or shall I hit you again?"

Charlie went on, stumbling and staggering. His head reeled. He could see no hope. He and Bill were outnumbered more than two to one. They were unarmed. How were they going to stop what was happening? And how was any miracle going to happen way out here? There was probably not another human for fifty miles. Except for Indians, and they didn't count.

Charlie reached the tree. Numbly he stopped and stood under the overhanging branch. And suddenly he was scared—worse scared than ever before in his life. He was really going to die this time. They were going to hang him. They would put him on his horse and secure the rope and whip the horse out from under him. The yank and the drop would snap his neck and he'd die like any murderer or horse thief swinging in the breeze.

He thought, "No! No, by God!" and turned to fight. But Martinez was there with his rifle posed to strike. He said savagely, "Go ahead. Give me an excuse and I'll bust your head open like a gourd."

Charlie forced himself to relax. He glanced toward Bill

and saw how close Bill was to putting up a fight anyway, no matter what the odds or the consequences of doing so. Briefly his glance met Bill's, and he quickly looked away lest Bill think he was asking him to help. Helping could only get Bill killed along with him and there was no sense in both of them dying here.

Conger said harshly, "Get his horse, Tolliver."

Tolliver went back and got his horse. He led it beneath the cottonwood limb and Conger said, "Get on him, redskin."

Charlie moved as slowly as he could. He moved as if in a dream, but even so it was only a minute or two before he was sitting astride his horse. Conger said, "Tolliver, throw your rope over that branch and put it around his neck."

Tolliver grinned. "It'll be a pleasure." He tossed the loop of his rope over the branch. Mounting, he rode close to Charlie and put the loop over his head.

Dismounting, Tolliver took the end and wound it around the trunk of the cottonwood. Martinez cut a switch from a nearby willow and walked toward the rump of Charlie's horse, looking expectantly at Conger.

Conger opened his mouth to give the order and Martinez drew back the branch. He stopped as Edith Roark's shaken and nearly hysterical voice said, "Drop that or I'll shoot!"

Conger said, "She ain't goin' to shoot. Whip that horse and let's get this over with!"

Martinez moved as if to comply. The rifle in Edith Roark's hands fired. Smoke rolled toward the group under the cottonwood.

Martinez collapsed to the ground with a shrill yell of shock and pain. The horse on which Charlie sat danced away.

He grabbed the reins, which had been tied up. Thank God, they hadn't tied his hands. Despite his efforts to hold the horse still, the noose tightened on his neck and pulled him back.

Slowly, slowly he gained control of the horse. He forced him back, choking until he was able to reach up with one hand and loosen the noose. Edith Roark's voice said shakily, "Let him go! Let him go or I'll shoot somebody else!"

Martinez was holding his thigh with both hands. Blood

leaked through his fingers. Tolliver released the end of the rope and stepped away from the tree.

Bill moved forward quickly, seizing a rifle from Savage. He ran to the tree and unwound the rope from its trunk. With the tension gone, Charlie lost no time in removing the noose from his neck and casting it aside.

He dismounted and picked up his rifle from the ground where Tolliver had thrown it earlier. He jacked a cartridge in, and looked at Edith Roark. Thanks seemed ridiculously inadequate for what she had done for him. He said, "Ma'am, I owe you my life."

"Just get away. Quickly."

Bill said, "Ma'am, you can't stay here. No tellin' what they'll do."

"The sheriff will see that nothing happens to me."

"Like he saw that nothin' happened to me? He ain't no better'n they are, ma'am."

She glanced at Savage uncertainly. Bill got his own horse and Savage's. He led Savage's horse to Edith Roark. "Get up, ma'am. Charlie's right. You ain't safe with them. Even if they don't hurt you, they'll leave you off first chance they get. At maybe some place like that last one we stopped."

That decided her. She took the reins he handed her and mounted with difficulty because of her skirts. Savage said, "Ma'am, don't go with them. They're outlaws now."

"Outlaws?" There was spirit in her voice. "Outlaws because they objected to being hanged? I will tell you this, Sheriff Savage. When we get back to civilization, I intend to tell the proper authorities just what kind of sheriff you really are."

Conger said, "Let 'em go. We'll catch up to 'em easy enough."

Savage hesitated just a moment more. Then he shrugged fatalistically. Bill said, "Ride out with Charlie, ma'am. I'll wait fifteen minutes or so until it's full dark an' then I'll come after you."

Charlie rode out, accompanied by Mrs. Roark. There was silence behind them except for Martinez's occasional groans or grunts of pain.

They were a mile away before they heard the rapid hoofbeats of Bill's horse behind.

He drew alongside and pulled his horse back to a walk. "They won't follow us tonight. Martinez's bleedin' an' they got to fix him up. But they'll be comin' after us tomorrow so we'd better make some tracks."

Charlie, earlier bathed with a cold and clammy sweat, was now chilled and shivering uncontrollably. He had looked into the face of death back there and it had shaken him as nothing ever had before.

To die in combat is one thing. To die by hanging, with everything done slowly and deliberately, is something else entirely. He promised himself that they'd never catch him off guard again.

Chapter 9

Everything was not, Charlie realized immediately, as simple as Bill had made it sound. Their horses were tired from three days of traveling. They needed rest. If they didn't get it, their weariness would make it possible for Conger, Savage and the others to overtake them tomorrow.

Charlie had no illusions left. He admitted that letting themselves fall into the hands of the men back there would be the same as giving themselves up to an executioner. Conger meant to kill them and Savage would not intervene. Being smitten with Edith Roark, he might try to hold out for *her* life. But she could be a witness against them once they got back to civilization and none of them could allow that. One way or another, she too would have to die.

They rode at a steady walk across the black and empty plain, Charlie in the lead, Edith following, Bill Waymire bringing up the rear.

Once, Edith Roark's voice came softly to Charlie's ears, "Where are we going, Mr. Waymire?"

Bill cleared his throat as if to answer. He stopped when he realized that the question had been directed at Charlie instead of at him.

Charlie turned his head. "I guess we hadn't thought ahead that far, Mrs. Roark. All we wanted to do was to get away."

"Are you still going to try recovering the boy?"

Charlie hadn't thought about that either. He opened his mouth to tell her he hadn't decided, but closed it abruptly. His ears had caught a sound and softly he called back to Bill, "Hear anything?"

"Horses. Comin' fast."

Charlie turned immediately at right angles to the direction they were traveling. He lifted his horse to a trot and

62

behind him Edith Roark and Bill kept pace. The sound of approaching horses' hoofs became louder and Edith Roark exclaimed, "I can hear them now."

Charlie said softly, "Don't talk. Sounds carry in the night." He reached a wide, shallow wash and rode his horse down into it. He dismounted and yanked his rifle from the boot. He did not, however, jack a cartridge into the chamber because he well knew how the sound of a gun action can carry on the still night air.

Edith Roark had also dismounted. She stood close to him, shivering. Bill remained on his horse, peering into the darkness.

The sound of horses' hoofs grew louder, then gradually began to diminish. Bill whispered, "They've gone on past."

Charlie said, "They couldn't have fixed Martinez up that quick."

"Nope. They must have left him behind."

Edith Roark gasped, "Left him behind? Bleeding and wounded the way he was?"

Bill said sourly, "You saw the way they killed them two Indians. You saw what they was about to do to Charlie. What makes you think they wouldn't leave Martinez behind?"

She was silent a moment. Then she murmured, "I suppose they would."

"Maybe they left somebody there with him. But I doubt it. They're short a horse."

"You don't think they left him without a horse?"

"Why not? He can hobble back to that buffalo hunters' camp. And if he can't, who the hell would care? He's only a Mexican." Bill's voice was tinged with bitterness.

"What are we going to do?"

"We'll go on in a little bit. Only we'll quarter north and maybe that way we'll miss that bunch."

They waited a while longer. Then Charlie mounted. Edith managed to mount without help, despite her skirts. Bill swung up last and they headed out, quartering north, riding at a walk. If they could save their horses, they might yet outrun the pursuit. Conger and Savage were spending their horses' strength recklessly in aimless pursuit through the night.

Charlie stared intently into the darkness ahead of him. At intervals he stopped and held his horse still while he strained his ears for sounds.

He dismounted once, in a little grove of willows on a dry stream bank. To Bill he said, "Maybe it's time we made up our minds what we're goin' to do."

"All right." Bill was silent after that.

Charlie grinned in the darkness. "You're layin' it all on me. Is that it?"

"You're the one with the most to lose."

"You mean I can't go back?"

"Not without that boy. Conger owns a heap of cattle and a lot of land. He packs a lot of weight. If you went back without the boy, he'd get you one way or another, no matter how long it took."

Charlie peered through the darkness, trying to see Edith's face. "What do you want to do, Mrs. Roark? I guess you've got something to say about this too."

"What are the alternatives?"

"Well, the only settlement ahead of us is Denver, and it's several days away. We might not get that far, because there are Indians between here an' there."

"And if we go back?"

"How safe you are depends on you, I'd say. If you keep still about all that's happened, maybe you'll be all right. Start stirrin' things up . . ." He shrugged in the darkness, not finishing. Edith Roark knew what he meant.

"What do *you* want to do, Mr. Waymire?"

It seemed strange to Charlie, being called Mr. Waymire just like he was white. He said, "It don't look to me like I've got much choice. I can't go back. And if we're goin' ahead, we'd just as well keep tryin' to pick up that trail."

There was a moment's silence. Then she asked, "You don't think I'll slow you down?"

"You haven't so far. Can't follow trail but just so fast."

"Then I say let's try and find the boy." She stopped a moment, then asked, "How do you expect to rescue him? There are only two of you."

Charlie had been wondering the same thing. He said, "We'll worry about that when we catch up with him."

He glanced toward Bill. "That all right with you?"

"It's all right with me."

Charlie mounted again and led out. The clouds had thinned somewhat, and the stars cast a little light upon the land. He put his horse down into a deep-walled wash, then climbed him out on the other side. Suddenly, ahead, he saw four horsemen less than a quarter mile away. Turning his horse quickly, he whispered, "Back down into the wash! It's them!"

Edith turned her horse back toward the wash. Bill's came scrambling out. He collided with Edith's horse while still only partway out. Losing his footing, the horse whinnied softly as he scrambled to regain it.

Out there in the darkness, the four horses stopped. Charlie said, "They've seen us. We got to make a run for it."

A rifle flashed, and another, and then the four horsemen were thundering toward them. Bill whirled his horse, put him back into the wash and spurred him recklessly along its twisting course, jumping obstacles and the roots of brush.

Edith had also turned. Her horse balked and Charlie hit it savagely across the rump with his rifle barrel. The horse leaped, almost unseating her, then slid into the wash and thundered after Bill, with Charlie close behind.

Where the wash grew shallow, Bill forced his horse up onto the level plain. Edith Roark came close behind. Charlie, glancing back, halted his horse, slid from the saddle and grabbed his rifle out of the boot. The horse went on a few steps, then halted uncertainly.

Charlie jacked a cartridge into the rifle. He knelt, resting the barrel on the lip of the wash. He knew that unless the pursuit was stopped, they weren't going to get away.

The four pursuing horsemen came on fast, having seen the shadowy shapes of horses climbing out of the wash. Charlie waited until they were less than a hundred feet away, until it seemed as if he would be overrun.

He drew a bead, then, as well as he could in the darkness, on the chest of the nearest horse. Actually, it was more like pointing the rifle than aiming it. It was a matter of feel, and he squeezed the trigger carefully.

The rifle shouted across the vacant land and almost instantly afterward, Charlie heard the distinctive "splatt" of the bullet striking flesh. The horse went to his knees, catapulting his rider on ahead, then somersaulted and then lay on his side, kicking helplessly and making a sound like a bellows with something in the orifice to make it rasp.

For an instant the man lay still. The others pulled

their horses up and Charlie heard Savage's voice ask solicitously, "You all right, Mr. Conger?"

There was an instant's silence. Then the figure on the ground sat up and his voice came harshly and caustically, "Am I all right? You dumb sonofabitch, what do you think? That goddam horse threw me for twenty feet. How do I know if I'm all right?"

"There's no call to talk to me that way," said Savage stiffly.

"I'll talk to you any damn way I please. Now help me up behind you and let's get that redskin sonofabitch!"

Charlie pointed his rifle carefully at the broadside view of Savage's horse. He fired again, squeezing off the trigger carefully. Once more he heard the "splatt" of the bullet striking, and once more he saw the horse go down. This one folded quietly forward and all Savage had to do was step out of the saddle as he did.

Belatedly, Conger bawled, "Back! Get back while we've still got two horses left! That damn Injun's tryin' to put us afoot!"

Tolliver and Jimmy Welch whirled their horses and spurred frantically back in the direction they had come. Charlie grinned, debating whether he should try for three. He decided against it because the light was too uncertain. And he wondered at himself. Why did he care whether or not he happened to hit a man? These were the men who would have hanged him back there a ways if Edith Roark hadn't intervened.

Maybe he just didn't have the killer instinct his ancestors had. Sourly he watched while Savage helped Conger to his feet. He brushed Conger off solicitously until Conger impatiently slapped his hands away.

Conger went to his horse, which was still kicking feebly. He shot the animal in the neck, then unbuckled the cinch and pulled the saddle off, no easy task because the cinch was under the horse's body.

Savage's horse was dead. He pulled his saddle off similarly. Charlie couldn't resist calling, "Good luck, gentlemen!"

Conger stopped and turned, "You dirty redskin bastard! I'll get you yet!"

Savage muttered urgently, "Don't provoke him, Mr. Conger! He'll shoot us like he shot the horses."

"Maybe we ought to just go after him afoot."

"You go, Mr. Conger. I'm gettin' the hell out of here."

Savage tramped away, his saddle bulky on his shoulder. Conger stood a moment, looking toward Charlie's hiding place. Then he followed suit.

Charlie walked to where his horse stood, mostly hidden by the wash. He mounted and rode in the direction Bill and Edith Roark had gone.

They wouldn't have to worry about Savage and Conger for a good many days. Maybe they'd never have to worry about them again. The two would have to ride double with Tolliver and Welch back to the buffalo hunters' camp. They'd have to haggle for horses, even assuming Conger had the money with him to pay for them. If he didn't, he might have to go all the way back home. Or he might have to try taking the horses they needed from the buffalo hunters by force. Charlie grinned to himself, thinking about that.

In any event, he and Bill and Edith Roark would have at least a forty-eight-hour start. In forty-eight hours, they would know whether they were going to find Danny Rutherford or not.

He touched his horse's sides with his heels and the animal broke into a weary trot.

Chapter 10

Charlie caught up with Bill and Edith Roark before he had gone a quarter mile. Their horses were halted and they were staring back toward him. Bill asked, "You all right?"

"Sure, I'm all right."

"What happened?"

"I shot Conger's horse and Savage's."

Even though he couldn't see, he knew Bill was grinning delightedly in the darkness. Bill chortled, "That must've been somethin' to see! Was Conger mad?"

Charlie grinned, thinking about it. "A little bit," he said.

Bill said, "Serves the sonsabitches right!"

They rode on silently through the night. Charlie wondered if he was ever going to find the trail again. He knew what the odds against it were.

At dawn, the three stopped in a draw where there was both water and firewood. Charlie gathered wood and built a small fire while Bill got the coffee pot. They had no food, having finished that yesterday, but the coffee helped. The sun came up, making the frost glisten on the grass. Bill stared across the fire at Charlie as he said, "There's only two of us."

"So?"

"I'd say let's forget about that kid. The Indians ain't goin' to hurt him none, an' it could be he's better off with them than with that grandaddy of his."

"We could head down into Texas. There's land down there—for the takin', I understand."

"You've already got plenty of land."

"Can't go back to it. Not now."

"We could if we found the boy."

"We ain't goin' to find that boy. We're headin' straight

into Injun country an' if we keep goin', we're goin' to lose our hair."

Charlie said, "*You* could go back. You're white. They wouldn't dare do anything to you. You could take Mrs. Roark along with you."

"Yep. I could."

"And even if you didn't go back, you could write to somebody and arrange to have your land and cattle sold for you. It would give you a new start down south."

"Yep. I guess it would."

"Then I'll go on. The Indians won't bother me. Not when they see I'm an Indian too."

"You might be dead before they can make out the color of your skin."

Charlie got to his feet and went to his horse. Edith Roark looked at Bill. "You're not going to let him go on alone, are you?"

Bill studied her closely, not answering. "What about you?"

"If you take the time to take me someplace you'll never find that trail again. Will you?"

Bill shook his head.

"Then I'll go on with you. That is, if you're both going on."

Bill nodded. "Let's get going then."

Charlie glanced back without surprise as Bill and Edith overtook him a hundred yards from the place where they had stopped. He did not comment. It was as if he had expected Bill to come. He had simply given Bill a chance to leave if he wanted to.

The sun rose behind them, warming their backs. By mid-morning they were sweating from its heat. Charlie now began quartering north, studying the ground closely as he rode. Plainly it had not rained as heavily here, and there was, once more, a chance of finding the raiding Indians' trail.

At noon, Charlie halted suddenly. He was staring toward the north and he pointed in that direction. "Dust. Somebody comin' toward us."

"Think they've seen us?"

"I doubt it. We ain't been raisin' much dust ourselves. Not like they are. I'd say there's twenty or thirty of them. Traveling at a lope."

"Indians?"

"Maybe."

"Then we'd better hole up for a while."

Charlie nodded. He went on, walking his horse now, looking for cover of some kind. It provided itself in the form of a low hill about a quarter mile ahead. Reaching it, Charlie dismounted and handed his reins to Bill. Afoot, he made his way to the top.

He could see the column of horsemen more plainly now, even though they still were more than a mile away. It was a column of cavalry, numbering forty-four horses in all. Of the forty-four, thirty-eight were ridden by troopers. The remaining six were pack animals. Charlie watched them long enough to ascertain their direction. Then he made his way back down the hill. He said, "Troopers. Thirty-eight of them. They have six pack horses and they're heading southwest."

"Where you reckon they're from? Fort Laramie?"

Charlie shrugged. "That's a long ways off."

He looked at Edith Roark. "You'll be safe with them, ma'am. No tellin' what might happen to you when we find the Indians we're looking for."

She nodded practically. But a rueful smile touched her mouth. "I guess I was looking forward to finding that little boy. But I don't want to make it harder for you than it already is."

Charlie took his reins from Bill and swung astride. "We'll intercept them, then." He rode out now at a steady lope, while the others kept pace behind.

They were still a quarter mile away when the cavalry commander spotted them. Charlie saw him raise an arm and saw the column halt. He approached at a steady trot.

The men looked worn and tired. They were sun-baked and dusty, mostly unshaven, and dressed in sweat-stained, frayed parts of uniforms. The only thing common to them all was the wide-brimmed campaign hat that each one of them wore.

Their commander looked little better than did his men. The only difference was that he wore a faded officer's tunic, upon which the insignia of his rank appeared. Charlie let Bill do the talking since the officer's stare was openly hostile toward him because of the color of his skin.

Bill said, "Howdy, Lieutenant."

The lieutenant touched the brim of his hat as he

nodded respectfully to Edith Roark. He said, "What on earth are you three doing away out here?"

"Trackin' hostiles, Lieutenant. They jumped a ranch three–four days back an' stole a boy. We lost the trail, but we're hopin' to pick it up again. What you doin' away out here, Lieutenant?"

"Routine patrol," the lieutenant said, his tone plainly adding that it was army business that he did not intend to discuss with them.

He was a gaunt man of about thirty-five, beginning to gray at the temples. A career officer, Charlie thought, who had probably been at least a major during the war.

Bill said, "Lieutenant, this here is Mrs. Roark. Her ranch was burned an' her husband killed by the same hostiles that took the boy. We'd take it kindly if you'd escort her back to your post so's she can make her way back to civilization safely."

"And you and the Indian intend to continue? Have you any idea how many Cheyennes are ahead of you?"

"Nope."

"Thousands. Literally thousands, sir. You haven't a chance of getting your boy back from them."

"We'll try anyway, Lieutenant. If it's all the same to you."

The lieutenant frowned at him. "Well, it's not all the same to me. I can't allow it. I'll have to ask you to accompany me back to Fort Lyon."

"Hell, Lieutenant, that's a hundred miles south of here."

"Something like that."

"You ain't got no jurisdiction over civilians, Lieutenant."

"I'm afraid you're wrong. My orders were to warn settlers and to bring in any who refused to leave."

Edith Roark glanced at Charlie and then at Bill. Quickly she said, "You an' your men look very tired, Lieutenant . . ." She paused, waiting for him to supply his name. He said, "Masden, ma'am. John Masden. And we are tired. We've been out almost two weeks."

Bill asked, "Had any trouble with hostiles, Lieutenant? I mean any skirmishes?"

"Fortunately no, since I only have thirty-eight men."

"You figure the Cheyennes are plannin' to attack the settlements?"

"I'm afraid I don't know what the Cheyennes intend

to do, sir. Now, if you will be good enough, we will resume our march toward the fort. Fall in behind me, please."

Charlie looked at Bill, and Bill shrugged helplessly. Lieutenant Masden indicated to Edith Roark that she was to ride at his side. Bill and Charlie let their horses follow along behind the pair. Charlie whispered anxiously, "We can't go all the way to Fort Lyon with him. If we do, we'll never find that trail again."

"Maybe it'll be just as well if we don't. If he's right and there are thousands of Cheyennes up ahead, then we stand about as much chance as a snowball in hell of stayin' alive, let alone of rescuin' that boy."

Charlie said, "Lieutenant."

The officer turned his head.

"There's some others half a day behind us. Four. Two of 'em are law officers. Without you to warn them, they'll head right into all those hostile Indians."

The lieutenant glanced at Bill. "That right?"

Bill nodded.

The lieutenant frowned uncertainly. "All right, then. We'll wait for them." He raised an arm to halt the column. To his sergeant, a burly, gray-haired man, he said, "We'll camp. I expect both men and horses can use the rest. Tell them they may have fires, but only small ones."

The sergeant nodded. "Yes, sir," he said, and rode away.

The men broke ranks. They dismounted, each looking first to the comfort of his horse. Saddles came off and wet backs were rubbed down with acrid-smelling gunnysacks. Bits came out and morrals of oats were hung over the horses's heads. A picket line was stretched between two poles. The pack saddles came off the pack animals and they were cared for similarly. Only when they had been, did the men turn to their own comfort.

Some gathered buffalo chips from a little grove of scrub trees. Others built fires. Pipes were packed and lighted. Some of the men stretched out and closed their eyes.

As soon as the lieutenant was out of hearing, Bill asked, "What do we do when Conger and Savage catch up with us?"

"Hell, I don't know. I didn't think that far ahead. All

I was thinking was that we had to get 'em to stop somehow. By night we'd have been twenty or thirty miles from here."

"At least the lieutenant won't go for a hanging. That's something anyway."

Charlie said, "We've got to get away."

"For God's sake, why? You don't owe Conger anything. And like I said before, that boy may be better off with the Indians."

Charlie said, "I guess it's hard for you to understand. I just figure that if I find that boy and return him to his grandfather, then maybe people will accept me."

"And that's important?"

"It's important. Maybe you don't think about it much, but then you've always been accepted because you're white."

Bill nodded. "All right. We'll see what we can do."

Chapter *11*

Sheriff Savage had watched helplessly as Charlie, Bill and Edith Roark disappeared into the gathering darkness. He knew, even before they disappeared, that he had made a mistake. He had sided with Conger and had not intervened when Conger tried to hang Charlie. Now the three were gone and it was too late.

He wasn't worried about Edith Roark's threat because nobody was likely to condemn him for letting Conger try to hang the Indian. Why, then, did he feel so wrong?

Unbidden came the memory of the young Indian brave and his squaw, who now lay unburied back there on the prairie. Indians they were. Hated Indians, probably guilty of raids and murder. But they were also human beings and they had been killed in cold blood and left to rot like animals.

Savage guessed what was bothering him was what he had seen in Edith Roark's eyes as she looked at him just before she left with Charlie Waymire and with Bill. He admitted that, despite the disparity in their ages, he had wanted her to like and admire him.

Conger now cursed bitterly as he stared in the direction the three had gone. On the ground, Martinez groaned with the pain of his wounded leg. Conger said shortly, "Savage, for God's sake, do something about his leg."

Savage felt a quick resentment. Conger ordered him around just as if he drew his pay from the rancher instead of from the county. Without comment, though, he knelt beside Martinez and began to cut his pants away from the wound. It was a clean wound. The bullet had passed on through. And while it was bleeding copiously, the blood came in a steady flow and not in spurts. Curtly he told Welch to build a fire and waited until he had.

"He can go back to the buffalo hunters' camp. He can

get a horse from them." Conger went to his saddlebags and dug out a small leather pouch. He took out five twenty-dollar gold pieces and stooped to hand them to Martinez. Martinez glared at them, then at Conger. Deliberately he spit in Conger's hand.

Conger straightened. Angrily, he threw the money at Martinez, then wiped his hand on his pants. A couple of the heavy coins struck Martinez in the face. The others hit the dirt close by. Conger muttered furiously, "You dirty Mexican sonofabitch!"

Savage said, "Give him a horse. We can get another someplace up ahead."

"To hell with him! Come on, let's go. I want that Indian!"

"And what about Danny? Have you given up on him?"

"No, I haven't given up!"

"How do you expect to find him now?"

"We'll find him. Someway or other, we'll find him."

Savage said, "I'm going back." He didn't know what made him say it. He wasn't going back.

Conger scowled at him. "Try it and I'll shoot you the way Tolliver shot that Indian."

Savage stared at the old man's face in the flickering light from the fire. It was grimly set and the eyes glittered. Something had happened to Conger in the last few days, he thought. Something had changed him. Grief, perhaps, over the loss of his daughter and her family. Anger and hatred for the Indians who had murdered them and kidnapped the youngest boy.

But it wasn't a selective anger and hatred, directed only against those who had committed the atrocity. It was hatred toward an entire race because of what eight of its members had done. And now it had extended itself to Mexicans because Martinez had dared get himself shot and had thereby threatened to slow them down. It would extend itself to him too if he continued to refuse to go on.

Savage said stubbornly, "He can take my horse. I'll double up with Welch."

"No! Damn you, Savage, are you goin' to do what I say or not?"

Savage suppressed his anger determinedly. If he continued to refuse he'd have to shoot it out with Conger and he didn't want to do that. Conger was still a grandfather, trying against hopeless odds to rescue a young grandson whom he loved. Savage had promised his help, and would not deny it now. Martinez could probably make it back to the buffalo hunters' camp all right. He could get a horse from them and make it home. Savage shrugged, "All right."

Martinez said unbelievingly, "You ain't really going to leave me, are you?"

"You'll be all right. I'll make you a crutch."

"He can make his own damn crutch," Conger said impatiently. "That Indian is gettin' away!"

Savage shrugged. He got Martinez's horse and mounted him. He didn't look at the Mexican. Neither did Jimmy Welch or Tolliver.

Martinez cursed them all bitterly, lapsing into Spanish. Conger took a moment to ride back. He said flatly, "Don't ever let me see your face again, you Mexican sonofabitch! I know what you just said to me!"

Martinez stopped cursing. He looked up at Conger silently. Conger turned his horse and rode away. Martinez spat after him with helpless viciousness.

From several hundred yards away, Savage looked around. Martinez had crawled away from the fire. He was barely visible, standing up and trying to break a branch from a scrubby tree to use as a crutch. Once more, Savage felt ashamed. But not for long.

Conger was riding fast and recklessly through the night but Savage knew there was little chance they would overtake the Waymires and Edith Roark.

He was tired and wanted to stop. The horses were also tired, and ought to have some rest. But he said nothing to Conger because he knew it would do no good.

They rode hard, circling and quartering, for almost an hour. At last Conger pulled to a halt. "Might as well make camp."

Savage heard a horse whinny and unexpectedly caught a glimpse of something moving up ahead. Conger saw it at the same time. He threw his rifle to his shoulder and fired instantly.

Savage opened his mouth to yell that Edith Roark was out there with Charlie and Bill, then closed it without doing so because he knew he would not be heard. Conger, Tolliver and Welch were firing indiscriminately as they galloped toward the dimly seen horses.

Savage spurred his own horse after them. The fugitives

had turned into a wash and were hidden momentarily. They appeared again where the wash grew shallow. Conger thundered toward them, closely followed by the other three.

Suddenly another rifle flashed. Savage heard the distinctive sound of a bullet striking flesh. Conger's horse went down, throwing the old man clear. Savage stopped to ask if Conger was all right and got an angry cursing for his pains. The rifle flashed again. This time the bullet struck Savage's horse in the side and the animal went to his knees.

Savage stepped out of the saddle. Conger yelled at Tolliver and Welch to get back out of range.

They did. There was no more shooting from the hidden rifleman. Savage said, "Well, that does it, Mr. Conger. We've got to get more horses before we can go on. And we ought to try and get more men."

"We do like hell!" Conger roared. "We'll ride double. But the horses need to rest. We'll camp and in the morning we'll follow trail."

The man was crazy, Savage thought. He'd get them all killed before he was through. Or maybe his determination would get his grandson back.

When night came, Charlie lay down as far from the fire as he dared, as close to the edge of camp as he dared. His horse had been grained along with the cavalry mounts. He was tied to the picket line, third from the end. There was one sentry over beyond the picket line and there was another on the other side of camp. The two paced back and forth, stopping to talk for a moment each time they met.

Troopers, exhausted by their long patrol, snored lustily. The horses fidgeted. Bill lay, apparently asleep, close enough to the fire to absorb its warmth.

Cautiously, Charlie eased his blanket off. Cautiously, he pulled on his boots. His rifle lay beside him and he picked it up as he came silently to his feet.

He reached the picket line in a score of silent steps. He spoke softly and soothingly to the horses, reassuring them. Reaching his own horse, he untied the reins from the picket line. He put the bit in the horse's mouth and rebuckled the throat latch. He didn't bother with the saddle, knowing that to try getting it would increase the risk of his getting caught.

Carefully, slowly, he backed the horse out, turned him and led him away. The two sentries' voices were barely audible as they talked softly at the ends of their posts.

From a hundred yards away, Charlie turned his head and looked back. Bill had turned over so that he now faced the direction Charlie had gone. Otherwise everything was the same. The sentries separated once more and walked back long their posts. The one between Charlie and the camp stiffened suddenly, staring toward the empty bed where Charlie had been only moments before.

His voice raised in an alarmed shout. "Hey! The Injun's gone!"

Charlie leaped to his horse's back. He drummed his heels on the horse's sides. Figures were running around back there in camp, silhouetted by the dying fires. Voices shouted, mingling so that their words were indistinguishable .

Charlie ran his horse for about half a mile. Then he drew him back to a walk. The horse was sweating heavily and stumbling occasionally.

Charlie traveled for another half mile, letting the horse's breathing become normal again, letting him cool off. This horse wasn't going to carry him indefinitely, unless he got some rest.

He was now alone. Hostile Indians were ahead. Conger and Savage were behind. He didn't know what Lieutenant Masden would do, but he would probably not give chase and would go back to Fort Lyon as he had planned.

He'd had no choice but to escape and he knew Bill would understand. He couldn't have risked letting Conger and Savage catch up. The lieutenant might not have countenanced a lynching, but he would probably not have refused a law officer's lawful request. And Savage would most certainly have insisted that Charlie be released into his custody.

As soon as he considered it safe, he dismounted. He had no picket rope, and he didn't dare let the horse run loose. So he dropped the reins and released the animal, himself squatting to rest and keep an eye on him. The horse stood for a while with his head hanging listlessly. Then he began cropping grass.

The task he had set for himself was an almost impossible one, Charlie realized. He grimaced ruefully in the darkness. If he had any sense, he'd go anywhere but straight ahead. There were a million square miles in which he could lose himself.

But he knew that he would not. In his way, he was just as stubborn as Conger was. He'd said he'd rescue Danny Rutherford and he'd keep trying until he did. Or until the Cheyennes took his scalp.

Bill watched the commotion in the cavalry camp with a half smile on his face. Charlie had done what he had expected him to and he was glad. Charlie couldn't be any worse off alone out there than he was right here. Masden was waiting for Savage and Conger to arrive and Charlie's danger from them was as great as any danger from the Indians.

Edith Roark walked to where he stood. "Will he be all right?"

Bill shook his head. "I don't know. But he couldn't wait for Conger and Savage to arrive."

"What are you going to do?"

"Depends on what Lieutenant Masden does, I reckon."

"Do you think he will go after Charlie?"

Bill shook his head. "I doubt it. No reason why he should. Unless . . ."

"Unless what?"

"Unless Conger and Savage show up before he pulls out for the fort. Unless they tell him a bunch of lies about what they're chasin' Charlie for."

"We could tell him different."

"Sure we could. But do you think he'd believe our word before he would that of a law officer?"

Masden came walking toward them. The men were settling down again. Masden looked at Bill and asked, "Do I have to put a guard on you?"

"Suit yourself."

Masden scowled irritably and thought it over for a while. Finally he turned his head and called the sergeant. "Put a guard on them," he said. Then he walked wearily back to his bed. He sat down and pulled off his boots.

Chapter 12

It was almost noon before Bill sighted the dust of the two heavily laden horses approaching from the southeast. One of the troopers, on guard, saw it at the same time and called, "Lieutenant."

Masden walked to him. The sentry pointed and Masden raised his field glasses and peered at the approaching cloud of dust. Turning, he said, "It's them."

Bill said, "They might have some pretty wild stories, Lieutenant."

"Like what?"

Bill shrugged. "I don't know like what."

"Who are these four? You never did tell me that."

"Rancher named Conger. Man that works for him named Tolliver. The sheriff and his deputy. Their names are Savage and Welch."

The lieutenant raised his eyebrows. "Sheriff?"

"Conger is the boy's grandfather and he's an influential man. The sheriff and his deputy came along to help him get the boy back."

"And your Indian friend?"

"He came along to track. I came to see that nothin' happened to him."

"Why would anything happen to him?"

Bill said, "Lieutenant, he's Indian for all that I raised him white. People hate Indians. All Indians. Conger even tried to hang him back there a ways when he lost the trail. That's when we parted company."

"How does it happen they're riding double?"

"Charlie shot two of their horses night before last when they caught up with us."

The two horses were closer now—less than half a mile away. Masden asked dryly, "Anything else?"

Bill grinned faintly. "Well, before that we passed through a buffalo hunters' camp. A young Indian and his squaw didn't like one of the hunters killin' buffalo for hides. Upshot of it was, Tolliver killed the Indian. The hunter tried to take the squaw an' she killed him. Then Conger killed the squaw."

Masden looked angry and irritable. He said shortly, "We'll wait and see what they have to say."

Edith Roark came to stand beside Bill. "What will happen now?"

Bill grinned. "Masden will have a hell of a time talking Conger into going back to the fort with him."

"Maybe he won't have to talk him into it. Maybe he'll just tell him he has to go."

Bill shook his head. "Masden will have to fight it out with Conger before he'll get *him* to go."

"And you don't think he will go that far?"

"Huh uh. I expect that the lieutenant will either let them go or will go with them."

The four men rode into camp, Conger and Tolliver on one horse, Savage and Welch on the other one. All four scowled angrily at Bill and at Edith Roark. They slid from the horses' backs. Conger nodded at Lieutenant Masden. "Howdy, Lieutenant. I'm Jake Conger. This here's Bart Tolliver. That's the sheriff, Savage, and that's Welch, his deputy."

Masden shook his hand. "And what are you doing out here, Mr. Conger?"

"Chasin' a murderer, that's what. Shot two of our horses night before last an' got away from us."

"What did he do?"

"Killed three people, that's what he did. My daughter, her husband, an' their oldest boy."

Bill said, "I told you it'd be some story, Lieutenant." Conger scowled at him.

Lieutenant Masden turned his glance to Edith Roark. "Somebody's lying, Mrs. Roark. Mind telling me who it is?"

Edith Roark said, "The story Mr. Waymire told you was true. Mr. Conger is lying."

Masden looked back at Conger. "Well?"

"Don't matter. Just turn the Injun over to us and we'll take care of him."

"I can't. He's gone."

"Gone? Where? When?"

"Last night. Mr. Waymire says he's still trying to locate

the trail of the Indians who kidnapped your grandson."

Conger snorted. "That's a likely story! After . . ."

Bill said, "After what?"

Conger didn't answer him. He said, "Lieutenant, I'd like to buy a couple of horses from you. I'll pay whatever you ask for them."

"I need all the horses I've got, Mr. Conger. Besides, I'm not authorized to sell government property to anyone."

"Damn it . . ." Conger stopped. For a moment he fought silently to control himself. At last he said, "Lieutenant, those Cheyennes have got my grandson. They killed his mother and father and older brother and he's all that I've got left."

Masden's face showed no sympathy. "Then you lied to me about the Indian . . . about the one who was tracking them for you."

Conger said wearily, "Yeah. I lied."

"Why?"

"Lieutenant, I buried my daughter and her husband and their son up behind the ashes of their house. I saw what had been done to them before they died. You can't blame me for hatin' Indians. Not after that."

"But Charlie Waymire was helping you."

"The hell he was! He just claimed to be helpin' us. All the time, he was holdin' back, an' sooner or later he'd have led us straight into an ambush."

"You don't know that."

"I don't? Didn't he deliberately lose the trail?"

Masden glanced at Bill, who said, "Who wouldn't lose the trail? It rained back there, regular gully-washer. Rained for a stretch ten or fifteen miles wide an' thirty–forty miles long. But I'll make you a bet. I'll bet Charlie will pick that trail up again before he's through. And he'll find the boy. Only how he'll rescue him all by himself I wouldn't know."

Conger said, "Just let us have a couple of horses, Lieutenant, and we'll go on. If you can't sell 'em to us, loan 'em. We'll return 'em to whatever post you tell us to."

Masden frowned uncertainly. Finally he said, "I've got to think about it. I'll let you know in ten or fifteen minutes, Mr. Conger."

Conger nodded, sure of himself. Masden walked away.

Conger stared at Bill. "You're gonna be sorry for crossin' me."

Bill looked backed at him sourly. "What'll you do, hang me?"

"Maybe that's what I ought to do."

Bill switched his glance to Savage. "And you'd let him, wouldn't you, Sheriff?"

Savage scowled but he did not reply.

Bill said, "One thing I'm going to do. When I get back, I'm going to tell the people who elected you just what kind of lawman they got for theirselves."

Masden came back. "I can't promise much, Mr. Conger, because my men are tired. But I'll give you a couple of days. If we haven't found your grandson by then, I'll have to return to the fort."

Conger nodded. "Thanks, Lieutenant."

Masden turned his head. "Sergeant!"

The sergeant, a stocky, weathered man, came toward him, his legs slightly bowed. Masden said, "Get two of the pack horses for these men. Most of the packs are empty, so you can double up."

The sergeant walked away, heading for the picket line. A few minutes later one of the troopers led two bare-backed pack horses to them. He handed the reins to Conger.

Tolliver mounted one, Welch the other. Conger and Savage mounted their horses, which had been standing with drooping heads nearby. Bill got his own mount and Edith Roark's from the picket line. He saddled them, then led her horse to her and helped her mount.

The troopers grumbled as they broke camp and saddled up. Edith said, "I didn't think he would."

"The lieutenant? I didn't either."

"Why do you suppose he decided to go with us?"

"It's within the scope of his orders, I suppose. Conger could stir up a hell of an embarrassing stink in the newspapers if he refused to help him rescue his grandson or if he refused him horses to do it for himself."

"He refused Charlie and you."

"He didn't believe our story."

"Anyway, he'll keep Conger from doing anything to Charlie when we do catch up with him."

Bill shook his head. "Don't count on it. What Conger wants to do he does. No matter who stands in the way."

The lieutenant led out, his sergeant riding at his side. Conger and Savage fell in behind. Behind them came Tolliver and Welch. Bill and Edith Roark followed them and the troopers brought up the rear. At the end of the column came the pack animals, plodding along wearily.

Apparently Charlie's trail was easy to follow because the lieutenant did not call for help. Like a dusty snake, the column traveled westward across the rolling plain.

Charlie Waymire held his horse to a slow walk all through the night. Occasionally he stopped and listened, while the horse listlessly cropped grass. Once during the dark hours he stopped at a narrow stream and watered the animal sparingly.

He wished he had some grain for him, but he did not. Nor did he have any food or blankets for himself. He'd have to kill something when daylight came, and he'd have to give the horse time enough to fill up on grass.

He felt more alone than he ever had. Stopping at dawn on a high bluff, he stared ahead, waiting until the sun touched the distant rolling hills. He was looking for smoke, the smoke of an Indian village, but he saw nothing.

Mounting again, he jacked a cartridge into his rifle and carried it cradled across his left forearm. He could take a chance on a shot, being far enough ahead of whoever was pursuing him and having satisfied himself that there were no Indians within hearing distance.

He had gone about two miles when his eye caught movement on a hill about half a mile to his left. He stared briefly. A lone buck antelope stood there, having just appeared from the other side of the low, rounded hill.

Charlie halted his horse immediately. He studied the antelope for a few moments more, satisfying himself that the animal had not seen him.

Mounted, there was no way he could approach unseen. He slid swiftly from the horse's back, and dropped the reins. The horse could graze but he would not wander far. Furthermore, it was only a matter of time until the antelope saw the horse. A curious animal, he'd study the horse, trying to figure out what it was. He would slowly approach, if nothing frightened him, until his curiosity was satisfied. If Charlie concealed himself between the antelope and the horse, he just might get a shot.

Carefully, he moved down the hill toward a dry wash at its foot. The wash was shallow and offered little concealment until it was an eighth of a mile away from the foot of the hill.

Charlie moved slowly and deliberately, making no sudden movements that might attract the attention of the antelope. He was also careful to move only on a course that took him directly toward the animal and not at right angles to that course. He finally reached a deeper part of the dry wash and was able then to almost completely conceal himself.

He crawled quickly now, on elbows and knees. Almost a quarter mile from his horse, he raised his head to look.

The antelope had seen the horse. His head was raised, ears pricked forward, and he was studying the animal intently. He took a hesitating step toward the horse, then another and then another still.

Charlie lowered his head carefully. He made himself comfortable. Now he only had to wait. If his horse remained reasonably still, cropping grass, the antelope was certain to approach close enough. His stomach began to growl in anticipation of antelope meat, broiled on a stick.

Chapter *13*

Charlie's shot rolled across the land, sharp and shocking in the stillness. The sound of the bullet striking the antelope preceded by an instant the animal's fall. He went to his knees, then collapsed quietly onto his side.

Charlie ejected the empty cartridge, picking it up, then scanned the horizons on all four sides of him. He stayed this way, motionless, for ten full minutes.

Finally he straightened. He walked to the antelope. He couldn't use all of the meat, but he knew that Bill and Edith Roark, if they had managed to elude Lieutenant Masden and were following, could use what he left.

He whetted his knife, then knelt and expertly gutted the antelope. Having done so, he skinned out a hindquarter. Laying it carefully on a clump of sagebrush, he propped the dead animal up on another clump so that it could cool.

Again he scanned all four horizons. Seeing nothing, he carried the hindquarter to his horse. The horse eyed the meat and laid back his ears. He fidgeted a little, but he let Charlie mount.

Charlie rode out at a trot, staying low until he had gone more than a mile. Then he climbed to the highest bluff around, and once more scanned all four horizons carefully.

The antelope hindquarter was hot and steamy lying across his knees. He was so hungry his mouth was watering, but he didn't dare stop and cook it yet. At a steady trot, he continued until the sun was a ball of orange low in the western sky. He halted in a place where there were a few willows, where there was a damp spot in an otherwise dry stream bed.

First he hung the antelope hindquarter from the branch of a tree to cool. Then he dug out a waterhole with his hands so that his horse could drink. The horse sucked up the water as fast as the hole filled. Charlie dug another hole and, while he waited for it to fill, gathered dry buffalo chips and built a fire.

The fire caught, sending up a thin plume of smoke that dissipated before it had raised twenty feet. Charlie hacked a couple of chunks of meat off the hindquarter, spitted them on sticks and arranged them over the fire so that they would cook.

Briefly the sky flamed, then died to the gray of dusk. The fire made a small and cheerful light. Juice from the meat dripped into it, hissing, sending out an aroma that would have been tantalizing even if Charlie had not been half starved. As soon as the meat had browned, he took it off the fire and put two more chunks on. Though the meat was almost raw in the center, he devoured it quickly the way an animal might.

He ate the second two chunks similarly. Then he filled his canteen, took a drink, killed the fire and lay down to sleep. He would be able to sleep without blankets during the early part of the night while the air was warm. Later he'd be huddled over the fire trying to keep warm.

The cold woke him sometime past midnight. He built up the fire and crouched over it, thinking of what lay ahead of him.

Dressed as a white man, he hadn't a chance when he reached the Republican where the Cheyenne villages were. He was armed, but the only ammunition he had was what was in his guns.

Only if he obtained Indian dress could he hope to survive. He might, perhaps, explain the shortness of his hair by saying he had cut it in grieving over a dead relative.

Having decided this, he waited no longer. He caught his horse and vaulted to his back. Drumming heels against the horse's sides, he once more headed west.

Dawn came gray and cloudy, cold from a wind whispering down across the plains from the high peaks of the Continental Divide. There was the smell of snow in the wind, and Charlie hunched his shoulders against its bite.

There was no sunrise. The sky was too heavily overcast. And a couple of hours after first light, it began to snow.

Uncomfortable though it was, Charlie knew it would help him. He stayed in draws and ravines whenever possible, and near noon he suddenly and unexpectedly heard a dog bark up ahead.

Instantly, he left his horse. He tied the animal in a steep-walled draw where he was almost invisible. He hung his hindquarter of antelope in a bush and cautiously followed down the draw. Occasionally he climbed its lip to peer out. The dog barked again, closer, and he heard a shout come faintly on the biting wind.

A Cheyenne village lay immediately ahead. Cautiously he approached until he could look straight down into it from the lip of the draw.

It was a small village, holding only eighteen tepees. It was nestled on the bank of a wide, nearly dry stream bed in the center of which a foot-wide trickle ran. Some children were playing in the stream, despite the cold and driving flakes of snow. A couple of squaws were walking along the far bank, gathering wood. The village could not have been here long, Charlie thought, or there would be no wood that close.

Uneasily he glanced behind him, not wanting to be surprised. He took off his hat and buried it in the dirt at the bottom of the draw. Clutching his rifle he waited. Sooner or later a man would leave the village and wander off alone. If one did not, he would have to go into the village after one.

He tried to make himself comfortable despite the bone-chilling wind. He shifted position so that the side of the draw would give him a little protection from its sweep. Shivering, he waited, as patiently as a cat waits for its prey.

The afternoon waned. Smoke began to issue from the conical tepee tops as fires were freshened in preparation for the cooking of the evening meal. Children disappeared into the tepees. Two boys walked upstream, probably to relieve the guards on the horse herd, Charlie thought. Ten minutes later two different boys came from the same direction and disappeared into the clustered tepees on the riverbank.

Charlie was, by now, chilled clear through. He was vastly relieved to see a man leave the village and come walking toward him.

The man was much older than Bill. His face was lined and dark, his nose prominent. Charlie regretted what he was going to have to do. He wished his victim might have been a younger man. Still, after waiting here all day, he could not afford to be particular.

The man passed him less than fifty yards away. Charlie glanced toward the village. It was now almost obscured by gathering darkness and falling snow. There still was no accumulation on the ground, however. The snow had melted as it fell.

Charlie eased himself out of the draw as quietly as he could. He was wearing white man's boots and he knew complete silence was impossible. The wet ground, though, would help.

He was still thirty feet behind the man when he was heard. The Indian turned, eyes widening slightly as he saw the shape rushing toward him through the snow. His hand went to his knife and his mouth opened to utter a warning shout.

Charlie hit him with a shoulder before the shout was out and the force of his body striking drove an explosive grunt from the man instead. The knife slashed through Charlie's coat and shirt and drew a rush of blood as it raked across his back.

But his hand now had grasped the Indian's wrist. He brought his rifle barrel down hard against the Indian's forearm and the knife fell from his numbed hand to the ground.

Charlie shoved the rifle muzzle into the Indian's belly. In Cheyenne he said, "Do not cry out, old one, or I will kill."

"What do you want? Your skin and face are those of a Cheyenne and you speak our tongue, but you are dressed like a white and your hair is short."

"I want your clothes, and I want to know if some young men with a boy captive have passed this way."

"And if I will not tell?"

Charlie prodded with the gun savagely. "Then I will kill you."

The old Cheyenne stared into his face a moment. Nodding, then, he said, "Eight young men with a captive did pass through our village yesterday."

"Where were they going? To what village did they belong?"

"They were from the village of Lame Bear. They said it was on the bank of the big dry river to the west."

Charlie guessed he meant the Republican. Poking the

Indian with his rifle muzzle to give emphasis to his words he said, "Go that way, old one, until I tell you to stop."

The Indian walked away, Charlie walked half a dozen paces behind him, his rifle cocked and pointed at the Cheyenne's back. He would kill the Indian if he had to, but not by shooting him. A rifle shot this close to the village would bring every warrior in it running to investigate.

Charlie reached his horse and meat. He gestured for the Indian to continue.

Not until a full half mile lay between them and the village did he permit the man to stop. The old Indian now looked fearfully at him. Charlie said, "I will not kill you if you do what I tell you to."

The Indian nodded.

Charlie said, "I must have your clothes. I will give you mine."

Nodding, the Indian took off his beaded deerskin pants, his moccasins and his deerskin shirt. Charlie took off his own clothes, taking care to keep the rifle within easy reach. He tossed them to the Indian, who was shivering in the cold. Charlie put on the Indian's clothes. Pointing to his horse now, he said, "Mount."

Charlie held the reins while the Indian leaped astride. Charlie handed up the meat. Then, holding his rifle, he vaulted up behind the Indian.

It was completely dark. Tiny flakes of snow drove along horizontally on the biting wind. The Indian asked, "Where are you taking me?"

"Far enough away from your village so that you cannot get back until I am far away."

The man nodded. After a while he asked, "Why do you wear white man's clothing and live in their villages?"

In English, Charlie said, "I'm damned if I know." In Cheyenne, he answered, "Long ago, white soldiers came to the village where I lived. They killed everyone and I was wounded but I got away. I did not know anything and was wandering alone on the prairie when a white man found me and took me to his house. He took care of me until I was well again."

"And so you stayed with him." The Indian nodded, satisfied. After that there was silence between them. The horse plodded along through the snow, which still had not begun to accumulate on the ground.

Charlie circled the old man's village and traveled for several miles before he let the old man slide to the ground. He realized that he was sorry to see the Indian leave. There had been little conversation between them. He had threatened the man and stolen his clothes. In spite of that, he had felt a strange friendliness toward the man.

The Indian disappeared into the darkness without speaking again. Charlie continued west, wanting to put a dozen miles between himself and the village before he camped. The snow would hide his trail.

He felt safer now. The only things to brand him white were the horse, the birdle and his short hair. He figured he could explain all three.

He knew he had been foolish to let the old Indian go. He should have killed him and hidden his body. Only in that way could he have made sure there would be no pursuit.

As it was, he could count on some kind of pursuit by warriors from the old man's village. Conger, Savage, Tolliver and Welch also were on his trail. It was possible Lieutenant Masden and his troopers were also following.

Maybe they'd come in handy when he caught up with the Indians who had Danny Rutherford. But, he thought wryly, they would probably be more of a danger to him than they would be to the Indians.

At midnight he found a low bluff and dismounted in the lee of it. He tied his horse to a clump of brush. He built a small fire and cooked several chunks of meat.

The fire died to a bed of coals. Charlie hunkered between the fire and the rock face of the bluff, miserably waiting for morning to come.

Chapter *14*

Masden halted for the night without having reached the place where Charlie had shot the antelope. The troopers scattered haphazardly, but out of their disorderliness came an order that was apparent almost immediately. A picket line went up. Morrals of grain went over the horses' heads. Fires were kindled with buffalo chips gathered from the nearby plain. Blackened pans were quickly arranged over the almost smokeless flames and bacon began sizzling in them. The smell of coffee filled the air.

Bill built a fire for Edith Roark and himself. He gathered a good supply of buffalo chips before he squatted down and accepted the tin cup of coffee she handed him. Conger, Savage, Tolliver and Welch had built their fire on the other side of the troopers' bivouac. Edith asked, "How much farther will we have to go?"

"Not far. The Republican can't be over a couple of days from here. I don't figure there's many Cheyennes beyond. Arapaho maybe, but not Cheyenne."

Edith's face was pale. "Will the lieutenant try attacking them to get the boy?"

Bill shook his head. "I think he's got more sense. Conger might do somethin', though, that would make it impossible for the lieutenant to stay out of a fight."

Edith breathed, "Thirty-eight men. Forty-three, counting Conger's men and you. Against thousands of Indians."

Bill did not reply.

"Where do you think Charlie is?"

Bill shrugged. "I don't know."

She seemed to want to talk. "What will *he* do when this is over with?"

"Depends on how it comes out. If he finds Danny Rutherford, he'll come back with us. He'll try making it as a white."

"And if he doesn't find the boy?"

"Then he couldn't come back no matter how much he wanted to. Conger would find a way to get rid of him."

"And the sheriff wouldn't stop him? Or even try?"

"He didn't try to stop that hangin' back there, did he?"

"It isn't right."

Bill grinned. "Right's got nothin' to do with it, ma'am. People out here ain't likely to forgive the Injuns for all that's happened for at least another fifteen–twenty years."

"There have been wrongs on both sides."

"Sure. This here is the Injuns' land an' we're takin' it. Folks feel guilty, so to make themselves feel better about it they downgrade the Injun in their minds. It's a sight easier to take land from an animal than it is to take it from a human like yourself. So they say Injuns ain't nothin' but animals. They say the Injun ain't usin' the land the way a white man would. Time they get through justifyin' themselves, the Injun comes out in the wrong."

"And Charlie still wants to go back and live with whites?"

"Yep. Charlie knows what's ahead for the Injun. The buffalo's near gone an' settlers are takin' up more land every day. Ten–fifteen years from now the Cheyennes are goin' to be penned up on a reservation someplace an' Charlie don't want no part of it."

She served him bacon supplied by the cavalry and hardtack, just what the troopers were eating. The fires died and most of the men settled down to sleep. Sentries began pacing the perimeter of the camp.

Edith Roark lay down to sleep and Bill lay down across the fire from her. He went to sleep almost immediately.

He awoke to a chill gray sky and a cold wind, on which were driven particles of snow and sleet. Shivering, he rebuilt the fire and crouched over it. He could see that Edith Roark was also shivering. After a few moments she, too, got up and came close to the fire to get warm.

They rode out in the same cold gray light, since this morning the sun was not visible. Conger, Savage and the others were silent, glum.

In mid-morning, still trailing Charlie because so far snow had melted as it fell and had not obscured the trail, they found the remains of the antelope he had killed. The lieutenant had it skinned, and had the meat loaded onto one of the pack animals. It wasn't much for forty-four, but it would make at least one meal.

Masden called on Bill to follow trail in the middle of the afternoon but it was almost dusk before he sighted the smoke of the small Indian village up ahead.

The lieutenant halted his men. Bill rode ahead to see how big the village was. Satisfied that it was too small to threaten the detachment of cavalry, he returned. Masden gave the order to move into it.

In a column of twos, riding at a slow and deliberate walk, they entered the village. Bill, who had learned a little Cheyenne while teaching Charlie the rudiments of English, acted as interpreter. Of an oldster, he asked, "Did an Indian dressed like white man come by here?"

The old man nodded and spoke to his squaw. She went into the tepee and came out, carrying Charlie's clothes. Bill turned to Masden. "Charlie must've jumped this old Indian and traded clothes with him."

"Ask him about the braves who had the kidnapped boy."

Bill obeyed. The old man launched into a swift stream of Cheyenne that Bill had trouble following. Helped by the old Indian's gestures, he finally understood that they had come by here, and that they still had the boy with them. Bill turned to Masden. "Charlie's following."

Masden looked at the sky. "Think you can still pick up his trail?"

"I can try but it's pretty dark."

"We ought to ascertain the direction he's taking if we can. By morning there may be too much snow on the ground."

Bill nodded. He rode out of the village at a trot. First he quartered north, then south, his eyes on the ground, a frown of concentration on his face. There were many trails this close to the village but he was looking for the trail of a horse wearing shoes. He found it finally, nearly a mile south of the village. He turned into it, urging his horse to a lope.

The snow continued, and the sky grew darker. At last, about five miles from the Indian village, Bill was forced to stop.

Masden stared around at the flat country. He glanced at Bill. "We've got to have a better place than this. If Indians should hit us, they'd cut us to pieces."

Bill gestured with his head. "There's a low bluff over there a couple of miles."

In the thickening snow and gathering darkness, it was, by now, impossible to see the bluff. Bill led toward it, but it was full dark before they climbed its sides and made camp on its top.

That night, Masden put out sentries on all four sides of the camp. He limited the fires to three, all built in a depression where their glow would not be a beacon to any Indians who might be on the surrounding plain.

Masden paced nervously back and forth, occasionally scowling at his thoughts. When Bill approached, he said, "Damn! I wish I was out of this."

Bill remained silent and at last Masden asked, "What do you think, Waymire? Will they hit us here?"

Bill shrugged. "Might. They know we're here. I'd be willing to bet that two—three young braves from that village back there followed us. Depends on how long it takes 'em to get help, I'd say."

"And there's a good chance that other villages are fairly close?"

"A good chance, Lieutenant."

"I shouldn't have let myself be talked into this."

Bill didn't dispute that because it was true. The Lieutenant *had* let himself be talked into pursuit of the hostiles who had kidnapped the boy, though, and it was too late to back out now.

"Lieutenant," Bill said.

"What?"

"Mind if I make a suggestion?"

"Go ahead. God knows I could use a few."

"Have the men build a few more fires. Let the Indians see. Then, three hours before daylight, slip away, leaving the fires and maybe a couple of horses you think you can spare. Lame ones if there are any. Time daylight comes, we can be ten—fifteen miles away. If it snows heavy, it might even cover up our trail."

Masden considered that. Then he said, "Good idea." He called his sergeant and gave the necessary orders. Several more fires were built. Two horses, going lame, were brought and tethered near the edge of the bluff where their silhouettes could be seen against the fire's glow.

The men lay down to sleep. So exhausted were they

that even the knowledge they would be moving out in about four hours didn't keep them awake. The fires died and were replenished, and died again. Once more they were replenished, near midnight, and allowed to die again.

Edith Roark awoke and looked up from her blankets. She was shivering. "What's happening?"

"We're movin' out in an hour or so. Before it gets light. The lieutenant figures them Indians back in that village might have sent for help."

She was silent for several moments. "We're not going to get out of this, are we?"

"I been in tighter ones than this."

"When?"

He grinned, hesitated and finally said, "Back there where Conger tried hangin' Charlie."

She looked away. Her shivering increased. He knew she was thinking of what had happened to her at the hands of the Indians when her ranch was attacked and her husband killed, but he didn't know how to comfort her, or even how to reassure her. She was right. There was a good chance they weren't going to get out of this. Like a rabbit surrounded by wolves, it was only a matter of time before they were run to earth.

He moved as close to the fire as he could get and pulled his blankets tighter over him. Snow sifted down slowly, beginning now to accumulate on the ground.

Bill dozed, and awakened, and dozed off again. Masden got up and began pacing nervously back and forth, occasionally stopping to peer fruitlessly into the darkness beyond the dying fires. At last he called softly, "Sergeant?"

"Yes, sir."

"Rouse the men. Tell them to stay away from the fires and not to build them up again. We're moving out, but it's got to be quiet or it's not going to work."

"Yes, sir."

The camp was roused, slowly and almost silently. Horses were saddled, the only sounds being the soft slap of saddle against the horses' backs, the softer sounds as a horse stamped a foot or tossed his head. In twenty minutes, the entire command had gathered on the western edge of the bluff, each man standing shivering beside his horse's head.

Masden called softly, "Mount. Quiet now."

Now there was a faint stir as the men mounted and moved on down the side of the bluff. The snow had dampened the ground, reducing the noise made by the horses' hoofs.

Bill could feel the flakes soft against his face. Edith Roark rode silently at his side, still shivering from the cold, or perhaps from nervousness and fear.

This way, they traveled for the better part of an hour. Flankers out on either side of the column reported no contacts with hostiles, and at last Masden ordered the command to trot.

This gait ate the miles and by the time dawn grayed the leaden sky, they were ten miles west of the bluff.

Staring back from a little rise, Bill scanned the horizon in a wide arc. He saw nothing even though the land by now was white.

He looked at Masden. "So far so good."

"But we still don't know where we're going."

"No, sir."

Conger and Savage rode to the lieutenant, Conger's eyes angry, his mouth a thin, straight line. "I take it he's lost the trail again."

"He lost the trail last night."

"And he hasn't picked it up again."

"Not yet."

"You tell him he'd better find it pretty damn quick if he knows what's good for him."

Disgustedly, Bill turned and rode away. He didn't want to listen to any more. Conger was stupid and narrow and bigoted and there was no use in even trying to reason with him.

Chapter 15

All morning, snow sifted out of the cold and cloudy sky. An eerie mist lay across the land, making it seem to Charlie Waymire that he rode alone in a void. He knew that this was more dangerous than riding when visibility was good. At any time he could come upon Indians, suddenly, and be seen himself before he had a chance either to hide or get away.

Sound first told him that an Indian village was near. He heard the faint barking of a dog, and a little later, a high shout that sounded as if it might have come from a child.

Immediately he began looking around for a place to hide his horse. Seeing nothing that would serve that purpose, he turned at right angles, knowing the village would be close to the bank of a stream, knowing too that above and below the village the stream bed would most likely have high banks and be lined with brush and trees.

He had gone no more than half a mile when he saw trees looming out of the mist ahead. He headed for them, gripping his rifle more tightly, as tense and wary as a stalking animal.

He reached the bank and put his horse down into the stream bed, feeling more secure almost immediately. In the thickest clump of brush he could find, he tied his horse and then moved toward the village, walking slowly and cautiously, stopping often to listen for the sounds coming from it.

There were always sounds in an Indian village and to Charlie they were suddenly familiar ones. The pounding of horses' hoofs as a couple of young men raced their ponies along the sandy, dry part of the flat stream bed. The ever-present barking of the dogs. The cries of the children and the scolding of the squaws. Sometimes the dull thumping of a drum, or the shouts of gambling men.

Walking slowly and carefully he nevertheless tried to avoid the appearance of stealth. Suddenly, looming out of the mist that lay over the stream bed, he saw a man approaching him. He pretended to pay no attention, but his body was as tense as it could be. The man was only a dozen feet away when he apparently saw how short Charlie's hair was. He stopped, half turned, his hand going to his knife. In the Cheyenne tongue he said, "Who are you? I have not seen you before."

"I come from the village of Stalking Bear." The name slipped out, and as quickly as it was out, he realized that all Cheyennes knew what had happened to the village of Stalking Bear fifteen years ago. But perhaps because this one was so young . . .

It was not to be. The Indian, a young man no older than Charlie was, said, "You lie. The village of Stalking Bear is dead. It was destroyed by the white soldiers fifteen winters ago when I was but a boy."

Charlie said, "That is where I am from. I have been living far to the east." He knew he was going to have to fight this Indian. The man had a knife in his hand and was hesitating only momentarily, trying to make up his mind.

Charlie said, "Take me to your chief. I have important news for him."

The young brave nodded. He started to turn and Charlie waited no longer, knowing this momentary advantage was all he was going to get. He attacked, swinging the rifle in a short arc like a club.

It struck the young Indian where neck joined shoulder instead of on the neck where Charlie had aimed the blow. It brought a sharp cry of pain, anger and surprise from him, and it also brought from him an explosive kind of reaction that made him whirl and slash viciously with the knife. Charlie arched his body to avoid the slashing blade but it cut through his buckskin shirt and raked his belly flesh anyway. He could feel blood, warm and wet, and hoped with a kind of quiet despair that the knife had not gutted him.

He had no time to investigate the wound, or even to put a hand there and feel to see how bad it was. The young brave came at him the way a mountain lion attacks a deer. Again Charlie swung the rifle, this time striking the Indian's forearm and making him drop the knife.

The Indian dived for it, seized it and rolled away, never stopping. He came to his feet half a dozen yards away. Charlie took this instant's opportunity to drop a hand and feel his belly where the knife had slashed. There was no bulge, just the wetness of fresh, warm blood. He felt the sudden weakness of extreme relief. The Indian rushed at him and Charlie parried instinctively with the rifle. He could kill this Indian by shooting him any time he chose, but in doing so, he would alert the village and bring a score of men running to see what was happening. The Indian's knife slashed the rifle stock, leaving a long scar, and nicked the back of Charlie's hand as it came away.

The pair circled warily. The Indian seemed to know that if he tried to flee he would be shot before he could get away. Between clenched teeth, Charlie said, "There is a small white boy in your village, is there not?"

The Indian made no response, no spoken one at least. But his expression gave him away. Charlie said, "I have come for him. And I have come to kill the eight young men who took him away."

This brought a fierce smile to the Indian's face. "Kill then," he said, "for I am one of them."

"You lie. You cannot tell me where he was taken from. Or what was done at that place."

"I can tell you. His father and mother and older brother were killed and their great wooden house was burned. And at another place between here and there another great wooden house was burned, a man killed and his woman used by all of us."

This Indian was indeed one of them, Charlie realized. And he had reached the end of his search. Danny Rutherford was in the village less than half a mile from here. He said, "The boy is still alive?"

"He is alive. But he will not be for long, once I have told the people that men from the white men's villages are here to search for him."

In English Charlie said, "You're not going to be tellin' anybody anything."

As if he had understood, the Indian attacked, leaping toward him with reckless savagery. Again Charlie parried with the rifle. The talk was over now. Now it would be a fight to the death and the Indian had plenty of experience at this sort of thing.

Charlie risked a glance toward the invisible village. The young Cheyenne laughed tauntingly. "They will be coming," he said. "And if you are not dead when they do, you will be soon afterward."

Charlie said, "Talk. Is that all the Cheyennes can do? Talk and make war on women and children?"

The taunt stung the Cheyenne. He leaped at Charlie, slashing with the knife. Charlie leaped back, but he felt once more the tug of the knife against his shirt. Off balance, the Indian staggered past and Charlie reversed the rifle and struck him with its butt.

The Indian took the blow on the shoulder, and let out a yelp of pain. Charlie lunged after him, following up his advantage. As the Indian recovered and turned, Charlie swung with the rifle, swung wide, holding it by the barrel.

It struck the Indian on the upper arm, the left one, and Charlie heard the unmistakable sound the bone made as it snapped. The Indian made no outcry this time, but his face turned gray as all the blood drained out of it. His eyes glazed and he stood swaying for a moment, dizzied by the pain.

Charlie wasted no time in sympathy and he worried not at all about fair play. This Indian had helped slaughter the Rutherfords. He had helped murder Edith Roark's husband, had burned her house, had raped her along with the seven others with him. He would kill Charlie unhesitatingly if Charlie did not kill him first.

Charlie swung the gun again, this time aiming at the Indian's head. Whistling as it came around, the gun stock struck the Indian on the side of the head with a sound that Charlie knew he would not soon forget. With his head caved in, the Indian was slammed aside. He fell and lay still, limp and looking almost harmless now that he was dead.

Charlie stood over him for an instant, breathing hard. He didn't dare leave the Indian here. He was sure to be found and his discovery would put the entire village on its guard. There would thereafter be no chance for Charlie to enter it and rescue Danny Rutherford.

Stooping, he grabbed the Indian by his deerskin shirt and dragged him into a clump of brush. Hurrying back, he brushed the unmistakable marks of the scuffle away with a branch torn from another clump of brush. Running, then, he went to where he had tied his horse. Still hurrying, he returned, leading the animal.

The horse didn't like the smell of blood, but after fidgeting uneasily for several moments, he at last stood still long enough for Charlie to boost the Indian's body on his back.

Voices from the direction of the village made Charlie's blood turn cold. Leading the horse with one hand, steadying the body with the other, he hurried away from the sound, grateful now for the shroud of fog laying in the riverbed. Several times he looked behind but he saw nothing and the sound of voices gradually grew fainter until at last it disappeared.

Charlie began looking for places to hide the body of the Indian. Without covering it completely, he didn't dare leave it this close to the village. A dog might smell it out.

Deciding that he was now as safe as he was ever going to be this close to the village, Charlie leaped to the horse's back behind the corpse. He drummed heels against the horse's sides and forced him into a trot.

He traveled this way for what he judged was half an hour, always keeping a sharp eye out ahead. At last, seeing a deep dry wash feeding into the riverbed, he turned. He rode his horse into the steep-walled wash for a couple of hundred yards. Sliding from the horse's back, he pulled the body off, letting it fall to the bottom of the wash.

The horse walked a few yards away nervously and stood looking back, trembling. Charlie rolled the body against the steepest side of the wash. Now he clawed at the wall of earth, pulling it down in great handfuls. When it got too hard to dig with his hands, he used the Indians's knife, which he had picked up back where the Indian fell.

Half an hour later, the body was covered with a foot of earth, hard-packed by Charlie's feet. He shoved the knife into the mound and covered it. Then he walked to his horse and mounted him.

His shirt was stuck to his belly with blood. The wound itself burned like fire but it had almost stopped bleeding now and wasn't serious. Except that the blood would attract attention to him, as would the knife slit in the shirt itself.

At the mouth of the wash he stopped. It was still daylight and he'd be stupid to try entering the Indian village while it still was light. The brave he had just killed had recognized almost instantly that he did not belong. Others would sense the same fact as quickly as the dead man had.

And if he was going to wait for dark, he might just as well use the time constructively. Bill was somewhere behind him and right now he could use Bill's help.

Accordingly, he climbed his horse out of the riverbed and headed back in the direction he had come, looking for his own trail so that he could follow it. What Bill Waymire could do to help him he didn't know. Neither did he know what he could do to rescue Danny Rutherford. But he had come this far and he intended to do something, even if he only got himself killed for his pains.

Bill picked up Charlie's trail in mid-morning, but he didn't tell anyone that he had. Instead, he put his horse into it, trying to cover it with the tracks his own horse made.

The trail was dim and indistinct, having sloughed off when the snow covering it had melted from the warmth of the ground. Nor was he absolutely sure it was Charlie's trail. He couldn't be sure of that without dismounting and examining it carefully.

Why he had instinctively concealed the fact that he had found the trail, he didn't know. Ruefully now he examined his reasons for doing so.

A superficial reason was that he hated to give Conger and Savage any satisfaction. But the main reason, he realized, was that he meant to slip away from both Conger and the cavalry if he got the chance. He and Charlie, unhampered either by a clumsy cavalry command or a vengeance-bent bereaved grandfather, might have a slight chance of effecting the rescue of Danny Rutherford.

And in doing so, they might save Lieutenant Masden's command from annihilation at the hands of the Indians. Outnumbered as they surely would be by perhaps more than ten to one, Masden's command wouldn't have a chance if they engaged the Indians. Rescuing Danny would make such an engagement unnecessary. Masden could retire, hopefully with his command intact.

But first, Bill knew he had to get away from the cavalry. And he wouldn't be able to do that until dark. Unless, by some unlikely chance, it began to snow again. Or unless a heavy fog rolled in.

Frowning, he kept his horse at a steady trot, wondering how far ahead of him Charlie was, wondering too how soon they would encounter some of the thousands of Cheyennes that he knew were camped in the vicinity.

Chapter *16*

At noon, Lieutenant Masden halted his troop. His expression was uneasy as he stared into the fog that had enveloped the column and the land surrounding it. He said, "I don't like it. In this damn fog, we could ride right into one of their villages and not know it until it was too late."

Bill asked, "Want me to scout ahead?"

Conger interrupted instantly, "Oh no, by God! You ain't going to get away from us that easy!"

Masden turned his head. "I am in command of this column, Mr. Conger, We are here at your request, but that doesn't mean you're running things." He looked at Bill Waymire. "Go ahead, Mr. Waymire."

Bill nodded, trying not to show the relief he felt. Conger grumbled and Tolliver muttered but Bill ignored them and rode away. The fog enveloped him almost immediately.

He kicked his horse into a trot, keeping his eyes on Charlie's trail but raising his glance frequently to peer into the fog ahead.

At this pace, he traveled for more than two hours. He wondered what Charlie had run into. He wondered if Charlie was already dead.

A figure loomed out of the fog and Bill raised his rifle instantly. He had a bead on the approaching Indian's chest and was tightening his finger on the trigger before he recognized Charlie and lowered it. Charlie halted his horse. "I've located him."

"Where?"

"Village about an hour away. Where's the lieutenant and his cavalry?"

"Back there. I left 'em to scout. How big a village?"

"Big."

"Too big for Masden?"

Charlie shrugged. "I never actually saw the village, but from the sound of it and the tracks, I'd say it was pretty big."

"But you were coming back."

Charlie grinned. "For you. I don't know whether two will be any better than one, but I didn't figure I had much chance going in by myself."

"And you're sure the boy is there?"

"He's there. I had a fight with one of the men who kidnapped him and he admitted it."

"You hurt?"

Charlie shook his head.

"I hope you didn't leave the Indian where he'd be found."

"I didn't."

Bill said, "Let's go."

"What about the cavalry? What will they do when you don't come back?"

Bill shrugged. "They'll either come on or go back. Hell, I don't know."

"Conger isn't going to let Masden go back."

"If Masden decides to go back, Conger won't have a damn thing to say about it."

Charlie knew they didn't have much time. Masden wasn't going to turn around and go back, at least until he knew what he was up against.

Bill said, "We got to find an Indian an' get his clothes. The minute one of them sees me dressed like this, he'll start blasting away."

Charlie wished he'd thought to strip the clothes from the Indian he'd killed. But he hadn't, and now it was too late.

Besides, he wasn't sure going into the Indian village would be smart for Bill. Bill's halting Cheyenne would be a dead giveaway.

But the uneasiness Charlie felt wasn't over that. He examined his own inner thoughts and decided that fear, either for Bill or himself, was not at its root. What was really bothering him was the fact that he had killed an Indian. By doing so, he had put himself irrevocably on the side of the whites. There could be no going back.

No moral questions were involved. The Indian he had killed had, himself, helped kill the Rutherford family and Edith Roark's husband. He might have killed other whites that Charlie didn't know about. But by killing him, Charlie had made sure he could never return to the Indians. And now he admitted that he didn't want to go back to them. He never really had. He liked living as a white. He wanted to go on living on Bill Waymire's ranch.

He also admitted to himself something he had not been willing to admit before. He wanted Edith Roark. After a decent interval, he wanted to ask her to marry him.

The course he had decided upon for himself was difficult. Only if he succeeded in rescuing Danny Rutherford would he have any chance of realizing it. Even then, things were going to be hard. He was an Indian and whatever he did or tried to do would be twice as hard as it would be for anybody else. Conger and Savage would see to that.

Bill was studying his face. Charlie grinned faintly at him. Bill said, "Looks like you've made up your mind about something."

Charlie nodded. "I guess you raised me too damn good. I don't want to go back and live with the Indians."

"Then we'd better get that kid."

No more was said. At a steady trot, the pair swept along through the fog. Eventually, near dusk, they reached the river bottom and put their horses down into it. Charlie said, "I could dig that Indian up for his clothes."

Bill nodded. "Better than taking the chance of tryin' to kill another one."

Nodding, Charlie led the way to the dry wash where he had buried the Indian. In darkness, he dug the body out and stripped the clothes from it. Bill changed, throwing his own clothes on the Indian's body before the two of them covered it again. The dead Indian's clothes were damp, but they'd dry off soon enough. Bill seemed to feel no particular distaste about wearing them. He looked at Charlie. "Now what?"

"We get close, I guess, and see how big the village is."

"All right. Let's go."

The ground was damp from the fog and the fog itself deadened the sounds they made. Leading their horses and traveling in single file with Charlie in the lead they approached the Indian village.

As they had before, sounds first let Charlie know how close the village was. A dog's bark came muffled out of the fog, and voices, so soft as to make the words indistinguishable. He whispered, "We're close."

Bill only grunted. Charlie whispered, "You stay here."

Bill started to protest, but Charlie stopped him. "If you hear a shot, come running. But don't do anything stupid. Don't get yourself killed."

Bill nodded. Charlie started away, but Bill reached out and gripped his arm. Their glances met, and held, and then Bill released him and Charlie moved away.

The enormity of the task he had set for himself was suddenly impressed on him as he entered the nearest village street. A dog sniffed at him, bristled, then moved away, growling deep in his throat, puzzled by Charlie's conflicting smells.

Where in the hell was he going to start, Charlie asked himself. He couldn't go from tepee to tepee, looking in. Nor could he wander indefinitely up and down the village streets without attracting attention to himself.

Somewhere, he could hear men's voices shouting a gaming chorus and dimly he remembered the game, in which a stick or "button" was passed from hand to hand on one side while the other side tried to guess in whose hand it was, all the while chanting in a high and minor key.

Despite the danger to himself, he felt strangely at home. The smells were familiar ones, coming to him out of his dimly remembered past, and so were the sounds. He stopped, and listened, a half smile on his mouth.

A woman came from a nearby tepee, lighted from the fire within as she opened the flap. She glanced toward him, unable to see him clearly because it was so dark. She spoke a soft word of greeting, which he acknowledged with a grunt, then moved away down the village street.

Frowning, Charlie walked slowly after her. There wasn't any way of finding Danny Rutherford. Not without questioning one of the village Indians.

He heard the woman coming back a moment before he saw her materalize out of the darkness ahead of him. She passed within a yard of him, and as soon as she had gone by, Charlie whirled. He encircled her throat with one arm and clamped the other over her mouth so that she could not cry out.

She struggled, but only half-heartedly, and let herself be dragged toward the riverbank, making no outcry. Charlie realized with a start that she thought he meant to drag her away from the village and rape her and she obviously didn't mind. A single woman, he thought, or a widow who was lonely enough to welcome even something like this.

Clear of the village, he took his hand away from her mouth. She giggled. He gripped her throat and the giggle died, to be followed by a sudden gasp of fear. He said, "There is a white boy in this village. I will kill you if you do not tell me where he is."

She began struggling now, frantically. Charlie tightened his grip on her throat, cutting off the air flowing into her lungs. She struggled harder, but his strength was inflexible. At last, starving for air and filled with fear that she was, indeed, dying, she began nodding her head vigorously.

Before releasing her, Charlie said softly, "Cry out and I will kill you before your second cry. Do you understand?"

She nodded her head even more vigorously than before. Charlie loosened his grip on her throat, ready to clap his hand over her mouth if she cried out. He waited for several moments while she breathed air into her starved lungs, gasping and occasionally coughing. When he figured she could talk, he said, "Where is he? I am going to leave you out here while I look for him. If you lie to me about where he is I will come back and kill you. Do you understand?"

Vigorously she nodded her head. He repeated, "Where is he?"

"In the lodge of Little Horse."

"That doesn't tell me anything. Where is the lodge of Little Horse?"

"It is in the center of the village, just behind the Medicine Lodge where the Sacred Arrows are kept."

"You know that I will kill you if you have lied?"

"I know." She was trembling.

There was only one way he could keep her here and quiet while he was gone. She seemed to know what it was, but she made no effort to get away as he raised the barrel of his gun. She winced even before it struck her, and afterward collapsed silently at his feet. The sound of the blow was dull because of the thickness of her hair.

He wondered if he had struck hard enough. He had tried not to strike too hard because he hadn't wanted to kill her with the blow.

He dragged her into some heavy brush and left her, in a position that would not cause her arms and legs to cramp while she was unconscious. Hurrying, then, he returned to the village, staying on the darkest of the streets, heading straight into the heart of it.

The Medicine Lodge was larger than the other tepees, and decorated more elaborately with various hand-painted designs. It stood by itself, the streets of the village radiating out away from it as the spokes of a wheel radiate out from its hub. There were several lodges that could be said to be behind it. Standing in utter darkness, Charlie tried to decide which one Danny Rutherford was in.

A man came from one of the lodges and disappeared. A baby began to whimper fitfully. A dog came to growl menacingly at Charlie, puzzled as the other one had been by his conflicting smells. Charlie ignored him, hoping he wouldn't start to bark.

The fact that his behavior was unusual seemed to increase the dog's suspicions. In a moment the animal was going to bark and that would draw attention to him. He had to move, now, if he wanted to avoid discovery.

Charlie crossed the small clearing toward the Medicine Lodge. He went beyond as if he had a definite destination. The dog, bristling and still growling softly, followed him.

Charlie whirled suddenly. He swung the rifle and heard it strike the dog. The animal yelped, a short yelp of surprise that died quickly, and slumped to the ground.

Charlie left him where he lay, going on, knowing he had to decide soon which tepee the boy was most likely to be in.

Back near the edge of the village, he suddenly heard a woman's scream. Almost immediately the village was filled with shouts. Men's shouts, women's cries, all asking what was the matter and who was screaming so. Dogs began to bark.

He hadn't hit the damn woman hard enough, Charlie thought. She had come to and in a minute she'd tell the people where he was and what he had come here for.

But he reaped one benefit from the woman's screams. An Indian and his squaw came from one of the tepee entrances ahead of him. The woman had a child by the hand.

The child was the size of Danny Rutherford. And as the firelight from inside the tepee fell upon his face, Charlie knew he had found the boy at last.

Chapter *17*

Danny Rutherford was dressed in deerskins. In the quick look he'd had at them as the firelight from the tepee flap illuminated them, Charlie had seen that the Indian couple were nearing middle age. Probably they'd had a child of their own about Danny's age, a child of middle age. Somehow they'd lost him and Danny had taken his place. They probably loved Danny far more than Jake Conger could. They probably would give him a better life than Conger would.

But judgments like who would be best for Danny were not Charlie's to make. His life had been on the line half a dozen times since Danny had been stolen by the Cheyennes. It was in jeopardy now, and so was Bill's.

The Indian ran toward the sound of the commotion, his rifle in his hand. The woman and the boy made dim shapes in the darkness near the tepee flap. Charlie sprinted toward them. With a sweep of his arm he sent the woman sprawling. He snatched up the boy and, carrying him under one arm, circled toward the place he had left Bill earlier. The boy began to scream with terror and Charlie clamped a hand over his mouth, stifling his cries. He said softly as he ran, "It's all right, kid. I'm Charlie Waymire and I'm taking you back to your grandpa."

He could hear the commotion started by the squaw coming toward him. He headed at right angles toward the stream, still with his hand clamped over Danny's mouth. He didn't trust the boy not to yell. A dog ran yapping at his heels and two others took up the chase. Charlie cursed softly to himself.

Suddenly, as he ran past one of the last tepees at the edge of the village, an Indian came from the tepee flap, a rifle in his hands. Charlie hit him with a shoulder and knocked him sprawling. He was lost in the darkness immediately, but behind him he heard the roar of the Indian's gun, and cursed again. Damn. That shot would bring the whole village running to this spot.

He was in the riverbed now, and he veered upstream, now taking his hand from Danny's mouth. The boy made no sound.

He passed the place he had left the Indian woman, glad she had not been hurt despite the fact that she had given the alarm. He was getting short of breath but he did not dare slow down. The brave at the edge of the village would point the pursuit north and south along the bed of the stream.

He wondered where Masden and his cavalry were. He wondered if they were camped close enough to have heard those shots. Probably not, but it was possible. In darkness and fog, Masden could have come quite close to the Indian village before he camped, without realizing it.

He saw Bill's dim shape ahead and heard Bill's voice call, "Charlie? Over here."

Charlie veered toward him and stopped, breathing hard. Bill took the boy from him. "How are you, boy? You hurt?"

Danny began to cry. Bill held him, and the boy put his face against Bill's chest. Charlie said, "Nobody hurt him. He's just scared. I'm not even sure we did him a favor by taking him away from them."

"If we hadn't, Conger would."

"Would he? Hell, Conger couldn't have gotten near to him. And there's enough Indians in that village to wipe Masden out."

"We'd better get back with him."

"We'd better get the hell out of here, that's a cinch." The two got their horses, mounted and rode out at a walk. Behind, they could hear the crashing of the underbrush as the Indians pursued recklessly.

Charlie knew the Indians couldn't follow trail. It was too dark. By morning perhaps they could be far enough away so that the Indians never would catch up with them.

The pair kept their horses at a walk for the better part of a mile. Then Bill urged his horse to a trot and at this gait they covered another mile. No longer could they hear any sounds behind.

Charlie called, "Bill?"

Bill stopped. The two horses stood close and Charlie said, "Are you heading back to where Masden is?"

"Yep."

"We'll lead the Indians straight to him."

"If we don't go back, Masden will ride right into the middle of them."

"Maybe not. Maybe he'd have better sense."

"Even if he did, Conger and Savage wouldn't."

"Am I supposed to care about them?" But Charlie knew they had to go back to Masden and the cavalry, back to Conger and Savage and the other two. He wanted to live like a white and that meant Conger and Savage and Tolliver and Welch. It meant putting up with them and others like them.

Bill kicked his horse into motion. The air was cold and damp and fog still lay close to the ground in places, drifting along the ground on a light night breeze. A bluff loomed up on their right and Bill called back, "It can't be far now."

Out of the fog ahead, shapes suddenly materialized. Charlie first thought they were the sentries around the cavalry camp but he knew he was wrong when he heard Tolliver's harsh voice, "Hold it! Stop right there or I'll shoot!"

Charlie stopped his horse and Bill followed suit. Charlie's hand was tensed over his rifle stock, but he didn't want to risk gunfire and so did not draw it from its scabbard. Gunfire now would not only endanger the boy; it would bring the Indians.

Bill called, "Put down the guns. We got the boy."

"You're a liar!"

"Come and see for yourself."

Tolliver said, "Go take a look, Jimmy. If they've got the boy, get him."

Jimmy Welch materialized out of the fog. Bill said, "Get back, Welch. We'll give him to his grandpa and nobody else."

Tolliver said, "You'll give him to us or I'll blow you out of your saddles!"

Danny suddenly began to whimper with fright. Bill said, "Easy, boy. Nothin's goin' to happen."

Charlie let his hand rest on the rifle stock. Incredible as it seemed, he knew Tolliver was going to kill one or both of them. Conger might have given him the order to do so without knowing Danny would be with the two. Tolliver could claim he had thought the two were Indians. And he'd get away with it.

Charlie swung his head and glanced at Bill. He wasn't close enough to see what Bill's expression was, since it still was dark. But Bill was facing toward him. Charlie said softly, "Now!"

Both men left their saddles instantly. Bill held onto Danny, drawing his revolver as he hit the ground. Charlie snatched the rifle from its scabbard as he left the saddle. He hit the ground on his back, the rifle having caught momentarily. But he had it, and he rolled away as Tolliver's gun flashed, as the bullet tore up a geyser of dirt less than a foot from his head.

Welch, who had been closer, was firing recklessly at Bill. Knowing any one of his shots could hit and kill Danny, Charlie ignored Tolliver for the moment and concentrated his attention on Welch. Rolling, he brought his rifle to bear, trying to pierce the fog and gloom beyond to be sure neither Bill nor Danny was in line of fire. Satisfied that they were not, he fired.

The bullet caught Welch in the back and drove him forward, instantly silencing his gun. Back toward the soldier camp, Charlie heard shouts from the sentries, and answering shouts from the troopers as they were roused.

Tolliver was also firing now. Another bullet flung up a geyser of earth, missing, but the one following did not miss. It tore through the muscles of Charlie's upper arm, bringing instant numbness and a warm, wet rush of blood.

Angered that he was hurt, Charlie rolled, once more trying to bring his gun to bear. Danny was screaming now. Welch was groaning and cursing bitterly. Charlie got Tolliver in front of his gun and fired instantly. He couldn't see his sights so he couldn't properly aim the gun. He could only point it, by feel, and hope his bullet found its mark.

He felt a sinking sensation when he realized it had missed. He worked the action desperately, jacking another cartridge in. This time he raised the gun to his shoulder and tried taking aim.

Tolliver fired again while he was doing so and this bullet grazed Charlie's ribs. Stung and further angered, he took careful aim on the middle of Tolliver's shadowy shape and squeezed the trigger off.

So close was he to the man that the report covered the sound of the bullet striking flesh. But he saw Tolliver go back, as though driven by the blow of some giant's fist. Tolliver struck the ground on his back, mortally hurt perhaps but not out of action yet. He sat up, raising his rifle again, pointing it in the direction from which the flash from Charlie's gun had come.

Charlie flung his rifle to his shoulder again. Tolliver was a brute, a stupid, animalistic brute, and he was as hard to kill. Tolliver's rifle and Charlie's racketed almost simultaneously.

This time, it was Tolliver that missed. Charlie's bullet took the foreman in the throat, and once more he was flung back as if by some powerful force. He lay on his back, spread-eagled in the mud, the fog swirled over his head, while the deep gray of coming dawn outlined his inert shape.

Charlie came to his knees, looking toward Welch again. The deputy was trying to get up, but all the fight was gone out of him. Bill was holding the screaming boy, having holstered his revolver now that there was no longer any need for it.

Out of the fog, out of the deep gray of coming dawn, Masden's voice roared angrily, "Tolliver! Welch! What's going on out there?"

Charlie shouted back, "It's all right, Lieutenant. We've got the boy and we're coming in."

He picked up his horse's reins and those of Bill's horse and led the two weary animals toward the cavalry camp. Bill followed, carrying the boy.

The troopers, some still in underwear, were drawn up in a line facing him. Their rifles were at the ready. Masden stood with his sergeant in the center of the line. Conger and Savage stood at his side.

Conger came forward to take the boy. His face was pale. His mouth worked and there were tears in his eyes. Danny went eagerly into his arms and threw his arms around the old man's neck.

Masden asked, "What was the shooting all about?"

"Tolliver and Welch."

"Shooting at you? Didn't they recognize you?"

Charlie said wearily, "Lieutenant, they've tried to kill me before. They were just doin' it again."

"Where are they now?"

"Tolliver's dead. Welch may be dead too by now, for all I know."

"Where are the Indians?"

"Close enough to have heard those shots."

Masden's face was alarmed. "How many of them?"

"Big village, Lieutenant. Too big for you."

Masden said, "Sergeant, roust out the men. We're pulling out."

"Yes, sir." The sergeant moved away.

Conger blocked the lieutenant's way. He looked at Masden incredulously. "You mean you're leaving? Without punishing those who killed my family?"

"You heard Mr. Waymire, Mr. Conger. He said the village was too big for us."

"You're paid to fight Indians! That's what you're out here for!"

"We rescued your grandson, Mr. Conger. Or Mr. Waymire did. Now we're going back. My men are worn out. The horses are worn out too."

"By God, I'll report you to your superiors!"

"You do that, Mr. Conger. You do just that. In the meantime, I'd suggest you get yourself ready to go."

Charlie watched the lieutenant stalk angrily away. He watched Conger turn and head for the picket line, carrying the boy.

The lieutenant was heading back, but that didn't mean there would be no engagement with the Indians. He was willing to bet that they were surrounded, even now, by Indian scouts. When daylight came and the scouts saw how small the detachment of cavalry really was . . .

No. It wasn't over yet. Idly he watched as two troopers headed toward the place where Tolliver and Welch were, leading horses on which their bodies could be loaded. The surgeon accompanied the two, carrying his bag, in case Welch was still alive.

The rest of the camp had suddenly become a beehive of activity. Charlie sat his horse, patiently waiting until they would be ready to go.

Chapter *18*

Dawn grayed the sky as the column moved out, heading toward the southeast where Fort Lyon was. It was a long way, over two hundred miles, and Charlie didn't think the Cheyennes were going to let them get away.

Edith Roark rode between him and Bill. She looked at him approvingly. "How in the world did you ever get that boy away from them?"

He said, "Sometimes it helps, being Indian."

Masden turned his head and glanced back at him. "How do you know Tolliver and Welch didn't mistake you for an Indian? You're dressed like one and so is Mr. Waymire."

"Because we talked to them."

"And they recognized you?"

"Sure they did. We told them we had the boy."

"And they still fired at you?"

"Yes, sir, They fired at us."

"You'll have to face charges for killing them. When we get back."

"Yes, Lieutenant. I expect we will *if* we get back."

Masden frowned. "You don't think we will?"

Charlie grinned faintly. "I think it's going to be disputed."

Masden stared around uneasily, his vision limited to about three hundred yards on account of the fog. "I wish this damn stuff would lift. We're sitting ducks."

"I'd put out flankers, Lieutenant," Bill Waymire said.

"Good idea. Sergeant!"

"Yes, sir?"

"Flankers to right and left. Tell them to range a couple of hundred yards ahead."

"Yes, sir." The sergeant let his horse drop back. Charlie heard him ordering men to take positions on the column's flanks.

Masden looked at Bill. "Any idea when they might take a notion to hit us?"

"They won't just yet. They need a little time to get organized. With luck, the fog will be gone by the time they do."

"But you think they will hit us, don't you?"

"I do."

Masden frowned. "I don't like giving them the initiative. They can lay an ambush and hit us where the advantage will be with them."

"Yes, sir. They can. And they will."

"Any suggestions, Mr. Waymire?"

"Yup. Let Charlie an' me snoop around a bit. If we can find out where they're goin' to lay their ambush, maybe you can turn things around."

Masden nodded. "Go ahead, Mr. Waymire. And good luck."

Bill kicked his horse into a trot and Charlie kept pace half a dozen yards behind. They disappeared into the fog.

Immediately, Bill turned his horse, avoiding the flanker on the left. He said, "This is goin' to be a picnic for them Indians. Best chance we got is to go back to their village an' see what they're cookin' up."

Charlie didn't say anything.

Bill pulled his horse back and peered closely at Charlie's face. "Havin' trouble makin' up your mind what side you're on?"

Charlie shook his head. "Nope. I might be Indian, but I wouldn't know how the hell to behave if I had to live with them."

"No reservations about fightin' 'em?"

"Not if they're fighting me. When someone tries to kill me, I don't give a damn what color skin he's got. I'm goin' to fight back."

"All right."

Charlie said, "Conger was glad to get that boy. Even if he couldn't bring himself to say thanks."

"Uh huh. I guess he was."

At a trot, they rode straight back in the direction they had come. The Indian village wasn't far. Maybe a couple of miles at most. They heard the commotion before they sighted it. Men were yelling. Horses were milling around. Squaws shrieked and children cried. Dogs barked incessantly.

Charlie grinned faintly to himself. It was like a picnic, or a county fair. It was like dogs on the trail of a wounded deer. They were going to make a celebration out of cutting Masden's command to bits. The braves would run them down and ambush them. The squaws and children would come along behind to watch from some not-too-distant vantage point.

Bill halted his horse. Charlie also halted his. Bill said, "Let's just tag along. Chances are, they won't spot us. If they should we'll make a run for it."

"Okay."

"You do the interpreting. I don't know their lingo well enough."

"So far, they're just getting ready. The kids have brought in the pony herd. They're getting mounted and milling around. Soon's they're all ready, they'll ride out."

"We're right in their path. Let's get to one side, and when they leave, we'll tag along."

Charlie rode his horse a quarter mile to one side. The voices of the Indians faded until no single voice was distinguishable.

The fog began to thin as the rising sun burned it off. The sun became visible as a luminous ball hanging low over the eastern horizon.

Charlie said, "They're moving out."

"All right. Let's fall in behind."

The murmur of sound passed in front of them and they followed it, keeping well behind.

They followed this way for half an hour. Charlie kept getting more and more tense because he knew they were between the attacking force of Indian men and the women, children, boys and old men who were coming behind to watch the show. He caught Bill's rueful glance. "We're a pair of fools," Bill said.

Charlie nodded. "Maybe."

"They're travelin' pretty fast. They ought to be ahead of Masden and his men by now."

Charlie nodded. "Trouble is, we don't know the lay of the land. We don't know what they're headed for."

"Canyon, probably. One they figure Masden will go through. They've got his route scouted by now and they know what direction he's headed."

Another hour passed. The fog thinned as the sun burned through it. Ahead, Charlie saw rough country covered with cedars and piñon pines. He didn't worry about being seen. They were dressed as Indians and their presence probably wouldn't even be questioned by anyone ahead of them who happened to spot them coming. The Indians' trail suddenly disappeared as individual braves scattered to right and left. Bill stopped his horse and the two of them stared at the entrance to a ravine. "That's it," Bill said.

Charlie studied the country ahead of them. It was no wonder the Cheyennes had chosen this spot for their ambush, he thought. On both sides of the ravine the land was exceedingly rocky and rough. The rocks would cover a trail and hide the ambushers. Moreover, it was so rough that passage over it was bound to be most difficult. The ravine offered an easier way, one that the lieutenant would not reject. He said, "This is as far as we can go."

"Yep. Let's go back."

Turning their horses, the pair trotted them back in the direction they had come, angling left to avoid the squaws and children coming to watch the battle. Charlie said, "If they avoid the ambush, the Indians will only set another one."

"And another one after that."

"Then what do you think the lieutenant ought to do?"

"Hurt 'em. Make 'em think their medicine is bad."

"That ought to suit Conger."

Bill nodded. He kicked his horse into a lope.

Following, Charlie admitted that Bill's answer to the dilemma was the only one that was practical. If Masden could somehow inflict heavy casualties on the Indians, even if only for a short while, then the Cheyennes would probably withdraw. They liked losses in battle even less than did the whites. When their losses were heavy, they believed the gods were against them.

Fanaticism in battle was almost completely unknown among Indians. They didn't fight to the last man. It was not their way.

A figure appeared ahead, a figure that turned out to be one of Masden's flankers. Immediately afterward the head of the column appeared, coming out of the thinning fog. Masden raised a hand and the column halted. Conger and Savage came from the rear and halted their horses at the lieutenant's side. Charlie and Bill rode up and Lieutenant Masden asked, "Find out anything?"

Bill nodded. Charlie remained silent and let him speak. "There's rough country five–six miles ahead. With a ravine leading through it. They're in the rocks on both sides of the ravine."

"We'll go around." Masden turned, preparatory to ordering the column to swing to the side.

Bill said, "You can do that if you want, Lieutenant, but it'll only work for a little while. They ain't goin' to give up on you. They'll lay another ambush somewheres else."

"Then what do you suggest?"

"Send a dozen men into the ravine. Send fifteen each to right and left to hit the Indians from behind."

Masden frowned. "My men are tired. They're badly outnumbered."

Conger interrupted, "What the hell do you think you're out here for, Lieutenant? You're here to fight Indians an' these are hostile Indians. The ones that burned my family out and stole Danny are with that bunch up ahead. It's your duty to fight them. If you don't, by God, I'll see to it you're courtmartialed for cowardice!"

The lieutenant's face turned a dark red. He said, "Mr. Conger, why don't you shut up?"

"I'm a citizen and a taxpayer. I got a right to let you know how I feel. You can bet I'll let your superiors know when we get to Fort Lyon."

Bill said, "Lieutenant, it's up to you. But them Indians ain't goin' to give up."

Masden nodded reluctantly. "Mr. Waymire, take Sheriff Savage, Sergeant Brown and a dozen men. Take them to the left of the ravine." He looked at Charlie. "You will go with me. Mr. Conger, you will also go with me." He called off the names of a dozen men who were also to accompany him. Brown was busily selecting those who were to go with him.

Masden called, "Corporal Weeks."

"Yes, sir."

"You are in charge of the others and the pack animals. Mrs. Roark will go with you. But you are to give us half an hour's start."

"What do we do, Lieutenant? When we're hit?"

"You retreat. You back out firing if you can, but you get out, no matter what. Is that understood? You will select a place to make your stand as you move into the ravine." He looked at Charlie. "Is there such a place?"

Charlie frowned. Then he said, "Gully that feeds into the ravine. Good cover there where it runs crossways for a piece. It's about a quarter mile this side of the head of the ravine."

Masden looked at Corporal Weeks. "Got that?"

"Yes, sir."

Masden studied the corporal, noting his nervousness. He said, "Do this right and you've got your sergeant's stripes."

Corporal Weeks tried to grin. "Yes, sir."

Masden said, "All right, move out."

Charlie led the way, heading off to the right. Bill led those with him away to the left. Corporal Weeks dismounted and ordered those with him to dismount. He pulled a large silver watch from his pocket and looked at it.

Charlie looked back once. Edith Roark, holding Danny in the saddle in front of her, was looking after him and when she caught his glance, she raised a hand.

He started to wave back, stopped when he caught Conger looking at him. Afterward, he cursed himself for letting Conger's bigoted stupidity stop him from doing something he had wanted to do.

Chapter 19

Charlie moved into the broken country an hour after leaving the others. Masden rode immediately behind him and Conger crowded Masden from behind, as if anxious to engage the Indians. Charlie thought ruefully that there would be enough Indians even for Conger in a little while, and he hoped Conger wouldn't do something out of eagerness that would endanger everybody. Masden's face was intent. The faces of his cavalrymen were stolid as if weariness had made emotion impossible.

Charlie knew, if Masden and the others did not, that everything depended on timing. The attack must be, first of all, a complete surprise. The casualties inflicted on the Indians must be heavy and devastating. Only if they were, would there be a chance that the Indians would disengage.

Charlie supposed he should feel like a Judas, but he did not. He had chosen to live out his life with the whites, even if most of them were hostile toward him because of his race. Whites and Indians were enemies. It was as simple as that. If he wanted to be a white, then he must fight with them as well as live with them. And if that meant killing Indians, then that was the way it would have to be.

They traveled through the rough and rocky country for another half hour. Corporal Weeks should be entering the ravine by now, Charlie thought. And he himself should have the ambushing Indians in sight.

But he did not. A touch of panic went through him, then went away again. He did not look at Masden or at Conger. Masden kept glancing uneasily at his watch. Once he asked, "How much farther, Mr. Waymire?"

Charlie didn't know. Shrugging, he said, "Any time, Lieutenant. Any time."

He wondered if he had, somehow, miscalculated what

the Indian position was. It didn't seem likely, but it was possible. He felt the sweat spring out beneath his arms and across his chest. He raised a hand and wiped his forehead.

Suddenly, immediately ahead, gunfire broke out, like exploding strings of firecrackers. Judging from the sound, it was less than a quarter mile away. Masden said sharply, "Corporal Weeks! They've attacked Corporal Weeks!"

Charlie was thinking about Edith Roark, who was with Corporal Weeks. He also was thinking about Danny Rutherford, as, apparently, was Jake Conger. Conger spurred his horse to the head of the column and yelled, "What the hell are we waiting for? Let's get after 'em!"

Charlie leaned toward him and seized his horse's headstall, pulling the animal up short. Conger reached instantaneously, swinging with his rifle barrel.

Charlie ducked, but he did not release Conger's horse. Masden said sharply, "Mr. Conger!"

Conger lowered his rifle sullenly without taking another swing at Charlie with it. Charlie said, "Lieutenant, if they see us before we're in range, the whole plan is spoiled. But we've got to get there fast or Weeks will have retreated out of range with the Indians following."

Masden said, "Go ahead."

Charlie veered right immediately, toward a shallow draw between two rocky hills. It offered them their only chance to approach unseen, and even this chance was slim. Still, Charlie thought, the Cheyennes would be intent on the little column in the ravine. They would have no way of knowing it was not the entire command. Masden's troop had been only perfunctorily scouted by the Indians and it was doubtful if the Cheyennes knew how many troops he had. Nor could they be sure they were not looking only at the column's head.

The firing continued, its intensity unabated except for an occasional lull while the Cheyennes reloaded. Other rifle shots, farther away, testified to the fact that Weeks was putting up resistance as he retreated down the ravine.

Charlie suddenly raked his horse's sides with the spurs. The animal broke into a gallop and thundered out of the little draw onto a hillside commanding the ravine.

Startled, the Indians turned to look as the command swept into sight. Frantically they brought their guns around and as frantically began firing.

Masden stood in his stirrups, turned his head and bawled, "Spread out to right and left."

The troopers executed the command as if it had been a drill. Masden, now only fifty yards from the surprised Indians, suddenly roared, "Dismount and fight on foot."

Immediately the cry went out, "Horse holders!" and those troopers so designated took the mounts from the others and led them up the rocky slope toward the rear. The others immediately knelt and began firing almost point blank at the demoralized Indians.

Charlie saw one go down before his gun. He saw others fall, some wounded, some dead even as they fell. Only fifteen white men in this group, he thought, and there must be at least a hundred Indians.

Already eight or ten were down, and still the devastating fire from the whites poured into them. Beside Charlie, a trooper lunged to his feet, his throat streaming blood. With a bubbling, inarticulate cry, he charged straight at the Indians, swinging his empty rifle like a club.

Across the ravine, Bill Waymire and Sergeant Brown suddenly led their troopers over the crest of the hill and attacked the Cheyennes on the far slope from the rear. Brown elected to keep his command in the saddle instead of dismounting them to fight on foot. The cavalrymen rode their horses down the rocky, precipitous slope straight into the ranks of the Indians, firing while their rifles still were loaded, swinging them like clubs when they had emptied them. The Indians, as surprised as those on this side of the ravine, got up from behind their rocks and sprinted for the floor of the ravine.

Charlie heard the bellow of Corporal Weeks, "Stand your ground, men! Lay it into them!" and the retreat of the small column stopped. They took cover behind what rocks there were and began firing at the demoralized Indians.

One Indian, tall and young, leaped out in front and began haranguing them. Charlie, despite the distance, was able to make out most of his words. He accused them of cowardice and told them they outnumbered the pony soldiers and could wipe them out.

Charlie, who had just finished reloading, raised his rifle

carefully. The range was close to six hundred yards. He allowed for a five-foot drop and squeezed the trigger off.

The bullet kicked up dust at the young Indian's feet. Quickly, Charlie jacked another cartridge in and raised his point of aim three feet more. Once more he squeezed off his shot.

This time he saw the Indian jerk as the bullet struck. Squarely in the chest it took him, and drove him back like the kick of a mule. He sprawled out on the rocky slope, clawing at the air a moment before he lay completely still.

Masden saw him fall and roared, "Keep firing! Don't let up!"

Renewed firing crackled along the slope and along the far slope where Brown's men were. The Cheyennes hesitated only an instant more. Then they retreated up the ravine, running from rock to rock. Conger roared, "After 'em! After the murderin' sonsabitches, boy!"

Masden's voice overrode the command. "Hold your ground. Let 'em go!"

Charlie walked back up the slope and got his horse. He mounted and let the horse pick its way to the bottom of the ravine.

Edith Roark was there, holding Danny Rutherford, who was big eyed but not crying now. Charlie looked at her from six feet away and asked, "Where will you go now? What will you do?"

She shook her head. "I don't know."

He said, "You can't go back. The house is gone, and a woman can't run a ranch by herself."

"*I* can, Mr. Waymire. If I put my mind to it."

He grinned at her tone. He noticed Savage watching them, a slight frown on his face. Savage also wanted her, he realized. But Savage would have to wait his turn to speak.

He said, "It don't seem decent to speak about it now, but later on, if you was . . . well, what I mean to say is . . ." He stopped, unable to phrase what he wanted to say so that it would not sound crude. She said, "I understand, Mr. Waymire, what you are trying to say."

He felt a vast relief. He said, "Come back with us. You can live in town. And there'll be time . . ."

"Yes, Mr. Waymire. There will be time." She looked squarely at him and quickly looked away.

Conger approached. Edith Roark rode away. Savage intercepted her and began to talk. Charlie watched the pair, noting her unsmiling face.

Conger said, "You turned it around by killin' that Indian."

"Maybe."

"That boy. You got him back for me. You risked your hide . . ."

Charlie looked steadily at him. "You trying to say thanks?"

Conger nodded with quick relief.

Charlie said, "You're welcome."

He watched Conger turn his head, watched him ride away. It had hurt the man to say thanks to an Indian, particularly to one he had tried so hard to hang. But Conger had tried until he got it said, and maybe that was the important thing.

Charlie looked toward the east, anxious now to get back home. Home. The word sounded good as it passed through his thoughts. Home was where a man lived, where he belonged. And Bill Waymire's ranch was home.